I0533637

Tales from the Canyons of the Damned Omnibus 11

PRESENTED BY USA TODAY BESTSELLING AUTHOR
DANIEL ARTHUR SMITH

For Susan, Tristan, & Oliver, as all things are.

35

Tales from the Canyons of the Damned

WARNING

HEARING PROTECTION REQUIRED

FEATURING

KJ KABZA

WENDY NIKEL

GORDON B. WHITE

PARASITIC MELODIES

PRESENTED BY USA TODAY BESTSELLING AUTHOR

DANIEL ARTHUR SMITH

Da Capo
Wendy Nikel

SILENCE FILLS the great hall.

A woman stands before the ivory and black keys, her fingers hovering in the still air. *There's no beauty without pain*, she thinks. But oh, how she's longed to hear the sound again. For years, she has kept her vigil in this great, empty room in this great, empty house in this world that's so vast and strange and silent.

She's kept the polished wood free from dust, free from scratches, free from the elements which would warp and weaken it. She's kept idle hands from dancing scales and arpeggios up and down its octaves, kept sticky fingers from slamming down its keys.

"Are you going to play today, Miss Grace?" her housemaid Isolde asks from the doorway, her face so young, so hopeful.

Even after all these years, the name sounds wrong in the old woman's ears. Grace. She'd chosen it for the grace note—a note melodically and harmonically nonessential.

"No, not today," Grace says, and Isolde's face falls in such disappointment that it makes the older woman hesitate.

She knows how her staff speculates about her, of her long-abandoned career in the opera and her obsession with the instrument in the great hall. They watch, every day, as she sits at its bench, resting her fingers gently upon the keys, her eyes closed, as if searching for a pulse. They speak in whispers that they think she can't hear: conjecture about why this instrument remains here, untouched; rumors about

1

how it's the most perfect instrument ever built and how the tone of its keys is like a heavenly choir; tales of how the piano and even Grace herself are not truly of this world.

How they've come to those particular conclusions is a mystery—suspicions passed down, perhaps, from those who'd walked these halls long ago.

"Isolde?" Grace asks as she rises from the bench. "Could you put on the gramophone? I'd like to have breakfast on the patio."

From the patio, she can't see those perfect keys, and with the outpouring of the gramophone in her ears, perhaps she won't be so tempted.

But her short shuffle to the patio is enough to make her wheeze, to make her lungs burn with exertion. This vessel which has served her for so long is growing weak, giving in to the ceaseless erosion of age and time. She's been guardian for so many years that the longing has reached a crescendo. It's a steady ache in her chest, like a note held impossibly long.

Just once before I die, she promises herself as Isolde sets the needle upon the ancient gramophone. *Just once, I want to hear it again.*

The gramophone shudders to life, pressing its cacophony into her ears. It fills the empty places within her incompletely, staving off the hunger but never fully satisfying. If only they knew what true music was.

Tonight, Grace thinks. It will have to be tonight, after the staff has departed, when the ancient old house is stilled of its rumors and whispers, and all that remains is her and the piano.

"That record all right, Miss Grace?" Isolde asks.

"It will do," Grace says wearily, "for now."

Grace remains awake far past the time when the grandfather clock strikes midnight. She sleeps very little these days. The silence, oppressive even in the daytime, is nearly unbearable at night.

It troubles me more now than when I was young, she muses as she makes her way down the spiral staircase, clinging tightly to the railing to keep from slipping. Then, the stillness had been a blessing, a welcome rest after all that had come before. But now, she finds herself thinking of the past more often, trying to grasp it like soap bubbles slipping through her fingers. She'd been warned that the day would come that she would regret what she'd done, but she hadn't believed it—hadn't thought it possible.

Already, guilt plagues her for what she will do, that which seems somehow fated and inevitable. Surely they'd forgive her if they knew it was her dying wish, if they knew how lonely it was here, alone, and how often she longed to hear their voices.

She draws in a ragged breath and positions her hands on the smooth bits of black and white. Her heart hitches, threatening to give out, and she pleads for it to hold on just a moment longer.

She lets her fingers press downward on the keys, and she feels for an instant like she's falling. Falling, falling, to somewhere else. To a world which was once so familiar.

G Prima stares up at the Chantress's palace through the shimmering white of her veil. The long, white building rises before the Seven Houses of the great City, spanning their length and looming over them with its perfect swirls and whorls, cut into its perfect walls of beech. Windows loom overhead, too high to see into. But perhaps not too high to scale.

"Go on, then, *Prima,*" a voice beside her says. Even with the white veil covering his face, G can sense the smile on her companion's face.

"I'll go when I'm ready, *Secundo,*" G says defiantly, not taking her eyes off the high ledge. "You cannot rush the music's tempo."

"*You cannot rush the music's tempo,*" Tertia mimics, laughing. "Come, now. I thought we were going to have some fun, yet here you are, quoting the musicmasters."

The musicmasters would be horrified if they knew their idea of "fun" involved sneaking into the Chantress's palace. If they're caught, they'll be demoted in their House for certain, and it'd taken G a lot of practice and dedication to work her way up to *prima.* But that's precisely why G has to try. To prove to her oldest friend that she's still the same, despite her place at the highest level of their House. To prove that she's still the girl he'd been younglings with: fearless and daring. To prove that they'll still be partners in crime, regardless of how high she rises.

The whorls carved into the beechwood are just thick enough for G to shove her fingers into. She reaches for the highest ones and lifts one foot in its silken slipper, trying to find a toehold. Secundo stands by, his arms crossed over his chest.

3

"You're supposed to be my lookout," G scolds him.

"I'm looking," he insists.

G pulls herself upward, her toes straining against their holds, careful not to snag her long, white robe. Step by step, she heaves herself upward, until her feet are at the level of her companion's head and she is within grasp of the lowest rail of the balcony.

She reaches out her hands, and her fingers brush the ebony rail.

Suddenly, the City Song, which rings out continuously in bright harmonics, weaving its way between the seven Great Houses, makes a sudden key change, a shift in the air itself, which no one could possibly ignore.

G loses her grip and slips backward. Secundo's arms soften her fall and he grunts as they both land on the polished wood street.

"What is that?" she asks.

He just shakes his head. All around them, other songsters bustle about, all flowing from their respective Houses in the direction of the city center, as their melodic voices rise and fall in curiosity and anticipation.

"The Chantress." Voices rise over the crowd's building song. "It's her summons."

A sense of thrilling trepidation fills G's heart.

"The Chantress?" Secundo echoes.

When was the last time the Chantress had graced the songsters with her presence? Certainly not in their lifetime.

They gather in the center of the city, on the steps outside the Chantress's palace — Primos and Ultimos and all those in between, from each of the seven great Houses and seven family lines. They pack themselves in as tight as hundred twenty-eighth notes on a scale, their voices blending with a quality of such flurried perfection and harmony that it stirs G to her bones. Younglings duck beneath people's elbows, and G feels a twinge of envy at the freedom to express their excitement they enjoy.

She peers over all the black and white hats of the fellow songsters, watching the balcony for the Chantress's entrance, for a glimpse of the enigmatic woman whom, all her life, she'd been taught to honor and fear, though she'd never been given a reason why.

"G!"

G spins at the sound of her mother's voice, her rich alto rising over the swell of the crowd. Mother's white robe is identical to G's own, and her face is draped in an identical veil, tucked in at the collar so that not an inch of skin is exposed.

"Mother?" G rarely sees the parents who'd raised her anymore, busy as she is in the Fourth House. Mother is of the Fifth, where G hopes to ascend, but G is no longer a child, and they each have their own duties to attend to. They each have their own song to sing.

G takes Secundo's hand and together, they weave their way through the crowd to reach G's mother, who offers a stiff, one-armed hug to her daughter and barely a glance to her companion. G freezes beneath her touch; how she'd hoped that things between them would change once she'd been accepted into the Fourth House.

Mother and Father had never bothered to hide the fact that G was the "difficult daughter." Their younglings preceding her had always done their lessons on time, always kept the perfect harmony of their household. Only G, their youngest, had ever questioned why.

Why must we wear these robes and veils? Why must we practice our tones? Why do we wear white while some wear black?

It's the way of our people, was their only response.

Father descends from the Third House as well: a white-suited man who places a gloved hand upon Mother's shoulder. His face, draped in a veil of his own, seems stiller than usual, and his crisp cap sits firmly, almost defiantly, atop his head.

He speaks in *pianississimo*, his tenor a drone in G's ear. "Are you still the Terza G of your House?"

Secundo nudges her playfully. She's been agonizing for weeks about how to tell her parents of her promotion, but now that the time has come, she's forgotten all the plans she'd laid out.

"I've been promoted," she says. "I'm the Prima G now. They haven't had anyone progress so quickly in generations."

Instead of the surprise and delight G had hoped would be their response, Father mutters something beneath his breath which is lost to even G's keen ears, and Mother reaches over to take his arm.

"It may not be like before," she says.

"You're right," he mutters. "It may be worse."

A tremor of unease shifts through G's body. "I thought you'd be pleased. What's going on?"

"I'm sure it's nothing to worry about," Mother says, her voice wavering in a way which G has never heard before.

"But the Silent Ones—" Father breaks off suddenly.

5

G had heard about the Silent Ones since she was a child—those ghastly creatures from the place beyond, who drove them into hiding so long ago. It's a tale told to even the youngest of younglings, a warning against those who would question or rebel. She glances at Secundo, who is holding unnaturally still.

Around them, their other Fourth House companions stand transfixed as the Chantress's melody swells in a crescendo. The older generations, too—their parents in the Third and Fifth, and grandparents in the Second and Sixth—clasp their hands and fix their unseen faces upon the balcony overhead. It is only the oldest, those hunched-over men and women of the First and Seventh Houses, that are not watching in awe. They stand at the edges of the gathering, holding one another, shaking their heads. G turns away, suddenly frightened.

Have the Silent Ones, those brutes, discovered them? Has something else—something worse—disturbed their peace?

One moment the Chantress is absent, and the next, she is simply there, her robes exactly like all the others but in a color G has never seen before. The shade is boldness and passion and anger and love and heat and power and a burning deep within her. It's beautiful and terrible to G's eyes and she can't help but stare.

And when the woman speaks, her voice embodies all that and more. "Once again, the time has come. We are being called upon to share our gift. To share our music. To share ourselves. Once again, the time has come to fulfil our duties."

Voices rise—minor chords, building fear and trepidation—but the Chantress holds out her hand and they fall in a *diminuendo* that leaves only the City's own song, comforting and constant, suspended in the air.

G's head jerks toward Father and Mother. She'd always known there'd had to be more to their toil and rules and training than what they'd been told. But what is all this about?

"Just give us the names!" a member of the First House calls out. His voice is so deep, it rumbles across the crowd, reverberating as others join in.

The Chantress waits for the crowd to hush before she speaks again, and when she does, it is with a voice of such authority that it is like many voices all together, a chorus resounding, an infinite proclamation.

6

"Three have been summoned—" she begins, and throughout the crowd, voices rise and fall.

"Summoned? What does she mean?" G asks Mother, but the older woman doesn't respond. "Mother!"

"—from the Fourth House."

G's heart patters faster in strange syncopation, and Secundo's hand finds hers. Father curses and Mother mutters what is perhaps meant to be a reassurance, "We knew it'd be the Fourth. It's always the Fourth."

"C Prima," the Chantress announces, "of the Fourth House."

From across the crowd, a Fifth cries out. A girl from G's House, wearing identical robes, is pushed to the front by gentle yet persistent hands.

Father grabs G's shoulders and spins her to face him. She feels the tremor in his voice, in his hands. "I'm sorry, G. We'd have told you if we could. We all agreed, the last time it happened. If our children didn't have to live in fear—"

"What are you talking about?" Secundo demands.

"E Prima of the Fourth House," the Chantress continues, and this time, the wailing cry compounds: a fugue of ugly dissonance.

Mother falls to her knees beside G, clutching her skirts and pleading with Father, "Don't let them take her!"

"G Prima of the Fourth House."

G's ears are too full. For the first time in her life, the music is too much and she presses her hands to her ears, trying to muffle the sound. The dissonance and discord.

Hands fall upon her. Secundo's are torn away. And somewhere above all the whirling sound, the City's tune still plays, growing louder and louder the more she tries to block it out.

How often had she dreamed of stepping inside the palace? But now, carried in by the rough hands and harsh rasps of the Chantress's guards—men and women with useless, toneless voices who've been deemed unfit to serve the great Houses—she wishes she was anywhere else.

Her eyes, wide with panic, cannot drink in the elaborate etchings or appreciate the luxurious swaths of smooth ivory and deepest, lushest ebony. Her ears, straining for the sound of familiar voices, can't bear the intricate cadences of the Chantress's song. Beside her, C has gone limp; the guards support her full weight on their gray-clad frames. E cries out questions that go unanswered, a keening in G's ear. But G herself remains silent, fighting to quell her fear.

The guards guiding C and E lead them in opposite directions, and G is alone, led into a room of such opulence and luxury that she finds herself even less capable of speech than before. One wall contains a window that looks out over the city, and the two adjacent ones are adorned with curtains of tiny droplet-shaped bells that tinkle in the gently shifting air. Sofas and curved-legged tables lounge beneath crystal chandeliers. Gently, she is guided to one of these sofas, one which faces the window, and her eyes transfix upon this strange and wonderful view as the black and white figures far below slowly— almost mournfully—disperse into the grand Houses of beech. She wonders which one is Secundo.

From here, she can see the markings carved upon the Houses' entrances, laid out in orderly fashion from First to Seventh. From here, their lives are but overlapping tones, rising and falling, dancing about, together creating something harmonious and perfect. Perfect and yet...what is this great secret they have kept from her? From the entirety of her generation?

The guards must leave silently, for the next sound G hears—which tears her from her inner thoughts—is the ring of the Chantress's heels upon the polished floor.

"Am I to assume that you are ignorant of your purpose here as well?" the Chantress asks.

"Yes, ma'am." G raises her chin, half-angry and half-fearful.

The woman in her strange, bold color sits beside G. "Do you know why we train within our Houses?"

"So that we might together create beauty."

The Chantress's veiled head bobs. "And what is the purpose of that beauty?"

G raises a shoulder. "For the enrichment of our lives."

"And that is where your elders have failed you," the Chantress says wearily, folding one hand over another. Her gloves are of the same strange hue as her robe. "What is a civilization that does not know its own history? That does not understand the source of its traditions or the importance of its duties? What hope do we have for the future if we don't heed the warnings of the past?"

G's mouth feels dry, her tongue sticky. In any other circumstances, she would have agreed with the Chantress. Now, that seems a dangerous thing to do. "What duty?"

"Did you know that we did not always live here?"

G nods. This story, at least, has been passed on.

"We once lived in a world beyond this one," G recalls, "among many other beings. Beings unlike us. Who didn't possess our gifts. For many centuries, we remained hidden, fearful of the Silent Ones. But then, we took a chance. We revealed ourselves and showed them our music. It entranced them, and we freely offered it up, for it pleased them so.

"But the Silent Ones grew greedy," G continues. "They were never satisfied with what we offered freely, so we were driven away into hiding once again."

"Have you heard it said, *there is no beauty without pain?*" the Chantress asks, standing to pace before the window.

"No." It seems an absurd sentiment, for they create beauty here each day and yet—save for the occasional accident—are free from any significant pain. Even at the end of their lives, the elders pass peacefully, their pain softened by the songs of their descendants.

"The Silent Ones killed us for one reason," the Chantress says bluntly. "Our death-cry."

"Death cry?" G's brow furrowed behind her veil. "I've seen people die—"

"You've seen the old die," the Chantress says. "Firsts and Sevenths perish with a whimper in their beds. It's only those who die a violent death who cry out. The Silent Ones killed us, slaughtered us young and old alike, just to hear the sound, for as lovely as our talking and singing and living and breathing sounds, the final cry of our people is like nothing else. It is stronger, more vibrant, and can cut through the thickest enchantments. It intoxicated them, drove them to crush us at any opportunity, and we knew we had to go back into hiding...or perish."

The Chantress wrings her hands in consternation. G watches, transfixed and befuddled at this revelation. Why had they kept this part of the story a secret? And what did it have to do with her?

"But we are safe now?" G tests out each word.

"It's not that simple." There is melancholy in the Chantress's voice. "We could no longer rely on our old hiding places, so we struck a

9

bargain with one of the Silent Ones—one who possessed powers unknown to us. He constructed this city, where we live in peace. But in exchange, when we are called—when we are summoned—we must answer. And now, we have been summoned again. You have."

"You need my song?"

"Your death cry."

G draws back, understanding striking her like a slap. "You'll kill me?"

"I will," the Chantress says calmly. "Within the hour. The bargain will be upheld, and our people will live on in safety."

"And I have no choice in the matter?"

"No. You were summoned by name. By your position."

"I never even knew about this bargain," G stutters. "You have no right to ask this of me. I won't do it."

"You won't?" The Chantress gestures to the window, where far below, the people mill about. "Not for the sake of all those? To keep them free from the terror of the Silent Ones? To preserve this beautiful world?"

G hesitates, staring down at the people below, drinking in the harmony of their song. When she turns around, still uncertain of her answer, the Chantress is gone.

Minutes stretch on as G is prepared for her ordeal. She is washed and perfumed and wrapped in fresh, new robes and a veil of expensive silk, and all the while, her mind searches for some escape. C and E join her before the Chantress's balcony, the curtain still closed tightly, yet with the gray-robed guards with their gray-handled clubs standing over them, neither dare respond when G tries to engage them in conversation.

"We don't have to do this," she whispers into their veils. "If we work together, we can break free."

"Don't be selfish," C finally hisses back, her voice already lined with pain. "You're not the only G of the Third House, you know. Would you rather your Secundo take your place?"

G goes cold. C is right. If G refuses her role as Prima G of the Fourth House, Secundo would be the one forced to take her place. She stares down at her feet, her heart raging with fury within her, cornered by this deal struck so long before her time.

10

The curtains open and the crowd stares up, their voices raised in their perfect song: a song, this time, of trepidation, of sorrow, tinged with self-loathing for what they are about to do. Three elaborate chairs—thrones, G might have called them before—await them upon the balcony.

The guards lead them each to a chair, and as the bonds of iron snap down against G's forearms, she knows that any chance of escape has passed. There is nothing she can do.

The Chantress steps up to her, tipping her head in G's direction. "I am sorry it must be like this. I know you hate me, but it is your parents who deserve the blame. I wish that they had been forthright about what must be done so that you might make this sacrifice willingly."

"I won't do it," G says between clenched teeth. She searches the crowd for her parents, but the robes and caps all look the same, so instead, she pretends that they all are hers. She can't bring herself to hate them, not when all they'd wanted was to protect her.

"My dear," the Chantress says, "you have no choice."

"You can kill me," G says slowly, contemplating each word carefully, "but you cannot make me cry out."

"There are consequences for such defiance, my child," the Chantress says softly, "for the balance must be kept. You're right, I cannot make you cry out, but I can warn you. Someday, you will wish you had."

And without another word of warning, it begins. Pain unlike any G has ever known courses through her body, lighting up her insides as though with fire. Every inch of her body—every hair, every nerve, every nail—cries out as if it will burst.

Beside her, C and E scream, their voices combining and reverberating through the air like nothing G has ever heard before as great tendrils of glimmering silver-thread are pulled from their bodies. The threads, once free, rise into the air, high beyond the Houses and archways, through the bounds of the City itself.

G presses her lips together tightly. She will not cry out. For her own sake, for Secundo's, for her parents, she refuses. They were all betrayed, long before they were born, and this blood-bought deal made her people no better than the Silent Ones, who'd barter with the lives of innocents. If she'd only known. If only there was more time.

The pain is ebbing...or is it simply her consciousness?

The death cries of her companions stretch on and on and on, until suddenly, there is nothing.

G stands before an instrument. Her hands, smooth and pale and uncovered, rest upon three ivory keys. She knows, somehow, though she's never seen this object before, the precise tones which she has pressed. Two still echo from the bowels of the box, yet the third key had depressed without a sound. Her key.

Around her, the world is strange and new. It is dark here, and still, and the only sound is that which comes from beneath her fingers. It is a bewitching sound, more perfect than anything she's ever heard. With a sharp breath of realization, she pulls her hand from the ivory keys.

Silence fills the great hall.

A Song Like Laughter
Gordon B. White

KATRINA HAD ONLY JUST BROUGHT Bradley back inside and set him on the floor when a burst of hollow rapping shook the front door of their trailer. She wasn't expecting anyone—friends were scarce, and her family hadn't visited since Bradley was born—and she hadn't heard the crunch of gravel in the driveway. Still, that didn't mean it wasn't Bradley's father, Joshua. He often dropped by unannounced and, sometimes, without his car if a bartender had taken his keys.

Bracing herself, Katrina picked up her heavy toddler and trudged beneath her burden toward the door. Even as she crossed the meager distance, another volley of knocking cracked against the thin door, and Bradley wailed. As she rocked him, Katrina stared at the broken tail of the chain lock that Joshua had shattered last month. Not for the first time, Katrina wished she'd gotten around to fixing things up.

"Who is it?" she called.

"It's me," replied a voice that rose and fell in singsong inflection. It sounded male, mostly, but the enunciation and the intonation vibrating through the thin particleboard were unfamiliar.

"Come on, darling," it sang again. "I don't have all day."

Katrina unlocked the door and slid it open just enough to peer through the crack, but there was no one waiting to meet her gaze. The yard and driveway were empty, too. She opened the door a little wider.

"Hey. Down here."

An enormous, gray and white bird squatted on the steps. Its head reached her hips and, from the tip of its hooked black beak to the end

13

of its flight feathers, it was almost as long as Katrina was tall. The snowy feathers on its breast burst against the thundercloud cowl of its head and wings.

"I thought you'd never answer," it said.

"Oh," was all Katrina could say. "Are you—oh." Her knees wobbled and the world fluttered as her vision dimmed.

"Hey!" the bird said. "Be careful!"

The bird's sharp words embarrassed Katrina out of her shock. She rooted herself to the ground and held Bradley tighter.

"What are you?" Katrina asked. She stared at the bird. "What are you doing here?"

"You know why I'm here, my dear." The bird's voice sparkled, dark and sweet. "Our deal is done and now I've come."

"Come for what?"

The bird cocked his head and blinked his bright yellow eyelids. From her angle above, however, it looked to Katrina as if he was winking.

"My son, of course." And he sang like laughter.

As the bird sang, Katrina's mind flew away, just a little, and when it returned, she was seated in a lawn chair, watching as the giant bird hopped around the yard. With its thick talons, it furrowed the ground then ran its scythe-like beak through the trenches. In Katrina's lap, Bradley strained against her arms, gurgling in wordless joy as the bird raked and pecked at the earth.

"I'm sorry," Katrina said, waking up to her surroundings. "But who are...Your son? Are you...Joshua?" She craned forward, looking for marks or scars that might reveal the man she knew—and sometimes loved—buried beneath the feathers.

The bird sang like laughter again. "No, no. Do you really not remember me?"

She shook her head.

"My name is," and he sang a trill that no human could replicate. "And we met back when, goodness, how old is he now?" *Trill* hopped towards them, pointing to Bradley with his beak.

"Bradley? He's two. Two-ish."

Trill stared. Katrina looked into his eyes but found only her own reflection in the storm-black sheen.

14

"He's big for his age," she said, unsure how to continue. She pinned Bradley's outstretched arms down and away from the bird's thick beak.

"Don't you wonder why that is?" *Trill* asked.

"His father—Joshua—he was big, too."

"My dear," *Trill* said, his voice lilting into a melancholy air. "Do you really need me to tell you a story you already know?"

She nodded.

The bird exhaled sharply, almost like a sigh. Then he sang, and the notes of his words flocked around Katrina, nestling her into a warm, mosaic film.

I was flying past one evening, skimming over the trees and into the purple horizon, when I heard you crying. The song of your sorrow was so sad and so bitter that I would have cried, too, if only birds had tears. I felt like it was raining and even the Earth's magnetic fields were being washed away.

And so, I had to land.

And I circled down to perch in the tree outside your window—I was smaller then, you see—and I watched you sobbing.

And there was a man behind you who was screaming, squawking, and he circled you, pecking, looking for an opening.

And then he flew away and the door slammed shut behind him.

And you were by the window, framed in the light from inside. You put your hands on your stomach, and you cried and you cried.

And I knew then. I knew what I could do for you.

So, I came back the next evening. You were alone but you were still crying. The air was heavy with salt and the sound of glass inside your home was like a wind chime.

I knocked on the door and you opened it. And you were out-of-focus, your eyes blurred beyond tears, but when you saw me there with my egg, you said it was as big as the moon.

And the glow from the porch light lit it as you held it in your hands, no longer trembling. The luster spread up across your arms and face and eyes and body.

And you said, looking through me and through the shell and through the light, you said, "I used to have one of these."

And I nodded.

"He might love me," you said, "if I had another."

And I nodded.

15

And I folded you within my wings and I told you, I said, "You could have this one, but only for a while."

You nodded.

"But one day," I said, "one day, I will come back for him."

You nodded.

And you picked it up, my still-not-born son, and you walked back inside. I watched through the window, watched you sitting there, pressing the vessel into your lap. You were holding the shell, just like you're doing now.

Katrina found herself once again in the dark mirror of the bird's glossy eye. She didn't remember how she got there.

"I don't know," she said. "It sounds familiar, but it seems," and she drifted off. As *Trill* had sung, the memories had built a nest around her; now that he had stopped, however, the stitches of her recollections were unraveling. But maybe, just maybe, it was like he said. Those had been such black days.

"And now, my dear," he spoke again, "I have to take him back."

"But you can't," she said. "You can't. I've kept him and I love him."

"And I thank you for that. But now it's time for me to take him. You can be free again."

"I don't think so. I don't know. I don't."

"Think of the open sky, the clear blue that awaits you."

"I don't want to be alone," Katrina whispered.

"But aren't you already?"

"But my son," Katrina said.

"My son," *Trill* sang.

The sky darkened between them as the sun dipped behind the tree line, spreading its shadow across the lawn like a great dark wing.

"You don't want this," he said, shuffling closer.

Bradley cooed and reached out his soft, pink fingers to rub the hard, black hook of *Trill's* beak.

Trill's breath rumbled softly as a new song, like some lullaby from a strange and distant country, crept from his tufted throat and wormed into Katrina's ears.

"You said it yourself, he's big for his age. But that's still albumen, and soon you'll see him change."

Katrina shook her head.

16

"Does he have all his teeth? No? That's because soon the points of his beak will protrude through his gums. And what you see now, these hen's-teeth, will fall to the ground like snowflakes of bone."

Katrina pulled Bradley closer to her into her lap. *Trill* sang on, the images fluttering behind her eyes.

"You'll see it soon," he sang. "Soon, the pinfeathers will sprout from his back. He'll itch and he'll scratch; he'll cry and you'll cry. You'll pull at the tiny bits, digging at them like weeds. But the roots will come out in clumps. And they'll bleed and they'll bleed."

Katrina shook her head again.

"And he's heavy now, you said it, you did. He is. But soon his bones will be thin and hollow like paper, his fingers stretching back to his elbows and his shoulders locking into new forms."

Katrina started to cry

"Has he started talking yet?" *Trill* went on, the air around Katrina roiling. "He won't, you know. Any day now, you'll hear him singing, to himself, like this," and *Trill* warbled. "It will be lovely. Until the next day or the next, when you stop finding it lovely. When his music has no words, not then and not ever."

Trill hopped and shook his feathers, the agitated rustling like bushes in a violent gale.

"And when the children, the neighbor children, and then the rest of the world begin to see how he is changing, whose son he really is, then they'll know." *Trill* croaked once. "Then they'll know what to do."

"What?" Katrina asked, bracing as if for a blow. "What will they do?"

"They'll take him. And cage him. Strip him. Pluck him. Scrape him. Open him up at the joints and—"

"Stop!" Katrina sobbed. "Stop."

Bradley had left her lap and was wiggling his way across the ground. The bird leaned over and nudged the boy with the curve of his beak. His scaled feet were large enough to carry Bradley, provided that *Trill* held him gently between his four toes. Seeing them so close together, Katrina couldn't detect the family resemblance, but children changed so much as they grew and she didn't even recognize much of herself, if any, in Bradley.

"They'll blame you," the bird said, lifting his wings as if to shrug. "They always blame the mother."

Katrina blinked again and again, but the images and lyrics from his story-song still drifted in her eyes.

"I, I know," she finally said. "I can't keep him, can I?"

"Nor do you want to," *Trill* said. He nuzzled her hand, clicking as he did. "But I need you to give him to me."

In a dream, Katrina walked over to where Bradley squirmed. She picked him up, kissed him quickly, then placed him down in front of the enormous bird.

"Can I go with you?" she asked, but she stared at the ground.

"No," *Trill* said. "I can't carry you both and you can't fly."

"Can't I just have a little longer?" She sank to her knees.

"No," *Trill* sang. "We have a long way to go and I'd rather not be late."

Katrina wept and tore at the grass. She clawed her nails through the dirt as his feet and tail feathers bobbed across her field of vision. She watched the broken leaves rise beneath the beating of his wings and saw Bradley's feet leave the ground, straight up and out of sight. His squeal of joy echoed through the clearing, spiraling out in the wake of their ascension.

They left Katrina beneath them, dark and small in the dying day.

"Da-da?" Bradley said, reaching up to the talons that held him high in the evening sky.

"Sorry, kid," *Trill* said. "But I've never seen you guys before in my life."

And he sang as he flew, sang like laughter.

18

The Deep Dark
KJ Kabza

I USED TO LOVE SITTIN' RIGHT there on the back porch, looking over the gulch at night, playin'. On a clear night with plenty a' moon, you can see where every hard-edged shadow and patch of light breaks off at the edge of the cliff, like splinters of a broken mirror.

Front porch was fine for playin', too. From there, though, other than the road, all you can see is forest. My Daddy used to call it "the Deep Dark". He first taught me to pick on that very porch the summer I was 7. "This here, this is the sound of the Deep Dark," he said, showing me where to squeeze on the banjo's neck with my pink, tender fingers. "An old, powerful sound. It's a piece of them trees. Wherever you play it, it'll conjure 'em up."

"What does that mean?" I asked.

"Bend your fingers more," he said.

I did everything Daddy told me to do with that banjo, same way his daddy had. Never thought to question it. It was just a thing our family did. Like how the Murphys were rich, and the Parkers were drunks. Us Smiths were pickers.

"If you do it real, real well on a clear night," Daddy told me many years later, "you might hear someone call back."

"Call back?"

He gestured for me to hand it over. It was Christmas Eve, 2005, a week before the mining accident and two weeks before my 19th birthday. We were sittin' on the floor in the living room, legs folded, admiring the tree that Mamma and the girls had decorated last night. "You know, call back—play a riff," said Daddy. His arms wrapped

19

around the banjo, and his fingers wandered and sang a Christmas hymn without thinking. "A little call and response, like. There are families hidden in the hills that are pickers, too." His expression turned funny. "Never managed it myself. But I heard them answer when my own daddy played, sometimes."

Monday after next, the explosion happened; by Wednesday, they found him down there, dead. Melody and Ashley, though old enough to be in college and working in the city, bawled like babies. Aunts and cousins and other family who hadn't bothered coming in, not even for Christmas, came now. I didn't bother with seeing them myself, though. I sat in my room and played, trying in vain to conjure him up from the deep dark.

I did that pretty much the whole winter.

Got good. Real good.

By the time graduation and summer came, my pain was like an old ache that came and went, buried under calloused fingertips, and there couldn't've been a better picker this side of the Cheat.

I knew it because one night, one of them answered.

I was playin' on the front porch, face to face with the trees, their rough trunks ugly and yellow in the glare of the porch light. Moths fluttered over my head, and now and then a bat would swoop down and nab one.

A slow, mournful melody twanged.

Didn't hear it at first. The Deep Dark is loud, summer nights, with crickets and katydids wailing. When I finally did hear it, I thought it was bullfrogs.

But then the insects shut up, and everything was black silence.

I heard it again.

Held my breath. Answered back.

It answered, and I answered, the notes in a minor key, uncomfortable to listen to. I tried to nudge the song along whenever it was my turn to play a variation, but the answer kept pulling it back to that haunting refrain.

Then the Deep Dark parted, and there it was.

It shambled out from the trees, lurching drunkenly on crooked hips. It was the size of a man, but no living man goes naked like this, with gray flesh sliding off the bones in flaps and ribbons. No man has eyes so tiny and black. No man has a mouth that takes up half of the face.

I choked. My fingers squeezed and the banjo shut up.

It stopped at the edge of the porch. A ribbon of its flesh lifted into the silent air, like a tentacle making a question mark.

We locked eyes.

When the next bat swooped down, the thing's ribbon lashed out and caught it without ever looking away from me. It lowered the bat to its wide gulf of a mouth. Bit its whole head clean off.

It chewed like a horse, lower jaw grinding in a wide, wide circle.

It swallowed. Then spoke. It parted its mouth just a shade, and while its gray throat bobbed and quivered, that slow, mournful song played out from between its narrowed lips.

I pissed myself and ran inside.

Mamma didn't believe me, of course. She thought I'd finally lost my mind. "I know you don't want to," she said, "but you really need to be around people again. Why don't you call up Joe or Scotty and go do somethin'?"

Instead, I stayed in the house. At night, even though I wasn't playing, I'd hear the wailing insects fall silent, and the sound of the thing in the woods around the house, calling.

Mamma found headless bats in the road.

On garbage day, I found a pair of headless raccoons by the garbage cans.

When poor Mamma found one of the Parker's dogs in the side yard, head missing and collar chewed off, I knew I had to do something. Me, I didn't care if I stayed in my room all day, but she was the one who needed to be around people, and she didn't deserve a fear that would keep her trapped.

I picked a night when the moon was gettin' full, when the sky was clear and the stars cut like slivers of glass. The July evening was cool and fine, and we had the windows open. By 9 o'clock, I could hear it calling.

By 10 o'clock, Mamma went to bed. I got out the banjo and tuned it in the living room. It had only been a week or so since I'd seen the thing by the porch, but it felt like a century. The old instrument's neck felt so right under my fingers, and I bit down on a flare of anger at that alien thing. My dad—he was the sound of the Deep Dark. Not that shambling monster.

When the banjo was ready, I put it in its case, strapped it to my back with some rope, and stepped outside.

The backyard was all stark moonlight and shade. I crossed it, slowing down as I got to the far edge. I grabbed a tree and carefully leaned over the sheer drop to the gulch. The moon was just right, and you could see all 96 feet of empty air. Where it stopped, the thin summer froth of the Middlefork glimmered between the bone-bright rocks.

I stepped back and swallowed. All the trees at the edge of the yard reach out over the gulch, fightin' for that swath of unblocked sky, so it was an easy matter to find a big Ash with branches that stuck way, way out over that long, long drop.

Not so easy to make myself climb it.

Even less easy to move out onto a limb that stretched over the void.

I couldn't go very far. Every little scoot along that branch made it wobble and bow, dipping just a little bit closer to that bone-brightness far below. The wood groaned. I clung to the branch like a clam, and I must've moved about as fast.

I made it to the branch's first fork. I tangled my legs in it tight, then fumbled off the banjo case and unbuckled it. My heart almost stopped when it lunged away, but by some undeserved miracle I caught it and clutched it back to me, using it to hold my ramming heart inside my chest.

In the backyard below, the crickets stopped wailing.

A mournful melody played.

I had to do this. I had to do this. I had to—

Before I knew it, my fingers were moving. I didn't even have to think. Just fell into the sound. It answered me, haunting and almost—oddly—beautiful, and surely, surely closer. I played again. It spoke again. My skin prickled with the ghastly wrongness of the duet. I'd been playing hard for a few months, trying in some way to conjure my dad. How long had this thing been speaking, waiting for an answer?

It shambled into the backyard.

Come on, I mouthed. Come on! It moved like a drunk, or like a wounded bird. Its flesh ribbons lifted and fell. Light and shadow rippled over its body as it picked its way through the trees, calling, calling.

It reached the edge of the cliff.

I played.

It took a step into nothing.

I don't know why, but I kept playing as it fell. Because I couldn't stop? Because I didn't want to hear that final sound? My eyes were closed, and I played my heart out, one long stitching-together of the duet we'd shared, some final attempt to make sense of the senseless.

When I stopped, the only sound was me, panting.

Why hadn't the crickets started back up?

I listened, I don't know for how long. Time loses meaning when you're jammed in a tree, some 115 feet over a dead alien.

Then I heard the call.

I stopped breathing. I couldn't make myself look below me, to check, but the sound wasn't coming from there anyway. It came from somewhere beyond the house, far to the north.

Then came another call, far to the south.

Oh God.

The Deep Dark resonated with the sound, a dozen calls or more, interlocking and harmonizing, like the howls of a wolf pack. Of course. How could I have thought that this thing was the only one of its kind?

I didn't climb down from that tree until dawn.

The Lost Tapes: The Q Mix
Daniel Arthur Smith

"RECORDING BEGINS WITH today's date, August 22nd, 2019. My name is Agent Melissa Muldoon. Present with me is Agent Lawrence Meyer. Commencing interview of one Dennis Davison—"

"Denny. Not Dennis. On my birth certificate, it's Denny."

"My apologies. My name is Agent Melissa Muldoon. Present with me is Agent Lawrence Meyer. Commencing interview of one 'Denny' Davison. Mister Davison is a DJ—"

"Curator. Not a DJ, a Music Curator. There's a difference."

"Again, my apologies. Mister Davison is a Music Curator and as such claims to have knowledge of the recent rash of suicides and extreme self-mutilations and their relationship to the Q Mix Playlist. He has agreed to this interview willingly. Mister Davison, can you please state your name for the record?"

"It's Denny Davison."

"I want to thank you for meeting with us."

"I believe in being helpful where I can."

"I noticed you have a subtle accent, but I can't quite place it. Larry said it's Swedish."

"Larry is right. I'm from Stockholm."

"Ha. Imagine that. Stockholm is lovely."

"You've visited Stockholm?"

"I passed through there once, on the way to a wedding in the north."

"In the summer?"

"Yes. It was lovely. The reception went late into the evening and it was still daylight. Quite amazing."

"Oh, the midnight sun. It is an exuberating thing."

"Yes. Yes, it is. Anyway. When you called, you said you had information pertaining to, in your words, 'incidents regarding the Q Mix Playlist'?"

"Yes. That is correct."

"And by incidents, you were referring to the recent rash of suicides and extreme self-mutilations?"

"Yes. Those are the incidents I'm referring to."

"And your assertion is that they are tied to what you've called the Q Mix Playlist?"

"Yes."

"Can you please describe the Q Mix Playlist?"

"Certainly. It's a curated collection of songs from various popular artists combined with layered ethereal soundscapes. Overall, the Q Mix plays like a soundtrack for life."

"Mister Davison, I have to tell you that Larry and I were quite curious to speak with you today. On scene forensics have found that the Q Mix Playlist is the one common link between the incidents. It's been found loaded on personal players, laptops, and stereos of each of the victims. But we haven't publicly released that information. So, the first thing we'd like to ask is how it is that you became aware of the Q Mix Playlist?"

"I couldn't tell you who started the leak, but when I stumbled across it, I didn't hesitate to reach out."

"And why is that?"

"Because I curated the media for the Q Mix, which is to say, I created it."

"In your role as Music Curator?"

"Um. Yes."

"And for my understanding, and for the record, just what is the difference between DJ and Music Curator?"

"People are often confused because there is a lot of overlap. Both DJs and Music Curators have extensive knowledge of music, and both are able to read their audience. But DJs are entirely in the moment. They're hired for a specific event or gig. The music's not usually saved or shared. They play their tunes and that's the end of it. A Music Curator, on the other hand, creates a soundtrack for life."

"You mean a playlist?"

"Not just a playlist. The perfect playlist. It could be for, you know? Could be a company, or a space, like a restaurant or club, or a person, like a celebrity, or maybe even an individual, like you. A Music Curator uses an understanding of lifestyle and music trends, science, market research, client interviews, all to create a perfect playlist that knows your moods, all the time, because a Music Curator isn't just curating music, they're curating an experience."

"And when you say curating, you mean you chose the songs and put them in a certain order. Like the mixed tapes my cousins used to make?"

"If your cousins utilized algorithms, layered signals, and psychoacoustics, then yes."

"I hardly think they did. Basic psychoacoustics maybe, but certainly no algorithms or layered signals. Could you please elaborate?"

"Well, it breaks down like this. The algorithms predict the desired psychoacoustic effect, that is to say how various sounds will be perceived. Additional signals, tones if you will, are then masked in hidden layers."

"Please describe what you mean by 'desired psychoacoustic effect.'"

"You mentioned that you've experienced the midnight sun. How did it make you feel?"

"Well. I felt spectacular. I didn't want to sleep, I had energy for days. I was— euphoric."

"That was due to all of that extra daylight, it affected your circadian rhythms—the physical and mental changes that correspond to your normal twenty-four-hour cycles of light and darkness. All of that additional light flooded your brain with serotonin and a ton of other natural chemicals and hormones."

"So, the light made me high?"

"Essentially. The change in cycles did, yes."

"But that was light, not sound."

"But you see, there are sounds that will do the same."

"So you create a list of songs that the algorithms tell you will create the optimal desired effect, and then enhance it further with subliminal messaging?"

"Essentially yes. But I assure you it's quite complex."

"I imagine. And just what is the desired effect of the Q Mix? Are you deliberately prompting people to harm themselves?"

"No. Not at all. At least, that wasn't our intention. I told you, I believe in being helpful where I can. The Q mix is supposed to induce focus through mood stabilization, the outcome of which should be the release of one's full potential."

"It sounds like you're taking the old adage 'music soothes the savage beast' to a whole new level."

"You know the poem?"

"Not really. No. Just music soothes the savage beast. Which sounds like what you're attempting to do."

"The poet William Congreve originally wrote it as, 'Music hath charms to sooth a savage breast, to soften rocks, or bend a knotted oak. All by magic numbers and persuasive sound.'"

"Magic numbers. A bit prophetic of algorithms."

"Indeed. But again, the Q Mix is supposed to help people."

"But these people didn't experience anything soothing or calming. Quite the opposite. The photos I have here show individuals who have performed lethal and severe mutilation, and on themselves, including tearing off flesh and muscles, disembowelment, and when that didn't immediately kill them, they continued to remove multiple abdominal organs. This man cut out his own kidneys. This woman carved her arm down to the bone. And this woman here sliced off her face and breasts. All of this from listening to your music."

"It's horrific. I'm not sure what happened. I mean, something obviously went wrong. I suspect there was somehow a corruption in the release of the signal. Perhaps if I could have a copy from one of the victim's actual devices—or the device itself. I could analyze it to determine what went wrong."

"That could be quite helpful. If you can excuse me for a moment, I'll talk to my supervisor and see what we can do."

"Hello, Director Higgins. You were watching from behind the glass?"

"I was."

"And what do you think?"

"Davison's a brilliant scientist. I figured he'd catch on to our tampering sooner or later."

"So what would you like to have happen? Is Mister Davison about have an accident?"

"No. He's too valuable to sacrifice. The audiological effects of the Q have worked a hundred times better than we could have anticipated. Colonel Ronson has already begun implementation of the Q in the field with great success. Unlike the BZ gas, the Q works on the individual. We don't need multiple enemy combatants to tear themselves apart if one will do the job for us. We'll be utilizing Davison's services in the future."

"And of Mister Davison's request?"

"Just give him an untampered copy. Let him spin on it."

"Will do, sir."

36

Tales from the Canyons of the Damned

BEWARE OF THE SCARE BEAR

FEATURING

STEVE ODEN
JESSICA WEST

KEVIN LAUDERDALE
KH VAUGHAN

PRESENTED BY USA TODAY BESTSELLING AUTHOR

DANIEL ARTHUR SMITH

Toys and Monsters
Steve Oden

FUZZY BEAR TURNED BLIND PLASTIC eyes toward the grumbling of an argument.

Toy Soldier apparently had set off Fairy Princess Doll again. Probably another chapter in their long-running dispute about social justice and mandatory military service. They never seemed able to resolve their differences when it came to the treatment of myth-biologicals and artificially-intelligent mechanicals.

Bear would have eavesdropped and found humor in their tiff. Both listened too much to radical left or right data streams, regurgitating the latest popular platforms and mantras. Neither espoused original ideas. They jousted with lances sharpened by political exaggeration and dipped in poison speculation.

But this was not the time for an escalating loud and senseless feud. He held up a paw and shushed the pair.

Although his organic eyeballs had been plucked out years ago, Bear's hearing was quite acute. He'd heard the whispered warning in his ear pod from Sock Monkey. The object of their surveillance—a higher-up intelligence officer who directed several anti-insurgency cells—had been spotted in a darkened window of the skid-row apartment building across the street.

Fairy and Soldier moved quickly to their assigned positions. He noted from the barely audible crinkle of dried leaves and street trash that this part of his team easily transitioned from political foes to deadly combat veterans who covered each other's butts.

Monkey had disabled the street light in front of the flop house that rented rooms by the night or week. She was the team's forward scout, her dark brown skin creped like fabric and flexible enough to slither in through a storm drain to escape detection. Her infrared vision, large red compound organs on the sides of her head like those of a giant insect, greatly aided in reconnaissance.

Bear's useless plastic button eyes reflected light, so he wore sunglasses. When the team saw him scratching the pilled fur beneath the earpieces, they knew the situation would soon get toasty. Giant Robot and Dragon covered the flanks and fire escapes. His shooter, Jack in the Box, was on the roof of the condemned warehouse on Bear's side of the street.

"Movement confirmed," Jack transmitted on the low-frequency radio link. "Can't be sure it's our target. They've got old curtains on the window, but somebody just walked past and made a shadow."

Bear pressed his throat microphone and asked if Jack could estimate the number of occupants in the room.

"Negative, but it's more than one. I picked up two heat signatures through the plywood sheet covering the other window, and somebody just flipped a cigarette out the open window."

Bear messaged the team: "Possibly three hostiles in the room. Jack can't get an exact number. We're going to presume three or four that need to be taken down. Stand by…"

Monkey was on the move, a nimble shadow jumping from a utility pole to the fire escape then scrambling up the brick wall. Soldier hustled across the street in full combat load-out, his stubby ten-gauge riot shotgun at port arms.

The urban assault vehicle fired up with a throaty burble of the 500-horsepower motor. Behind the wheel, Fairy was strapped securely in the crash seat, ready to roll at Bear's signal. Jack wouldn't have anything to do except provide cover fire after the snatch and grab, if everything went as planned.

"Monkey's inside," Jack transmitted.

"Count off 30 seconds for her to get in the room above the target and set the charges. Robot and Dragon, you're the uninvited guests who will drop in through that big hole in the ceiling."

34

Robot buzzed, "We are ready and skippy, boss." *Zzzzzz.*

It would be crowded in the room with those two brutes jostling for position.

He started the countdown on the team band: "Count is now T-minus fifteen seconds, fourteen, thirteen..."

At the eight-second mark, all hell broke loose. Every remaining window in the dilapidated structure blew out in gouts of fire and smoke. Monkey screamed, the sound etching painfully over a chalkboard in his mind. A heavy-caliber automatic weapon steadily thumped. This was not the plan. The opposition had been tipped off and laid an ambush.

"Pull out, team! Fairy, bring that battlewagon up. Help Jack. Repeat, haul ass out of there..."

The roar of Dragon's flamethrower was savage music to Bear's ears. The fire-and-brimstone was already eating through the structure. The entire building was only minutes away from collapse.

Soldier's riot gun cycled through a drum magazine of slugs, chewing the locked steel entrance door to pieces and blasting scrap high in the air. He disappeared inside and seconds later, reappeared to hurtle down the steps with a bleeding sock puppet slung over his shoulders.

Bear couldn't see with his plastic button eyes, but he could hear Robot lumbering through the ground-floor hallways, laying waste to plaster walls, furniture, and enemy gunners with his laser blaster.

"Dragon's out, Robot's right behind him," Jack announced. "All teammates are accounted for." He began picking out targets of opportunity in the smoke and systematically triggering the depleted-uranium slugs from his .50-caliber sniper rifle. Screams and curses were silenced when the super-high velocity rounds punched through bone and soft tissue to blow holes in brick-and-mortar walls.

The heavily armored assault vehicle roared down the street, remote-controlled chain guns purring like deadly kittens and mortar tubes chuffing anti-personnel bomblets and smoke grenades. Fairy had the back hatch open and waiting. She expertly maneuvered the fighting machine to form a protective barrier for retreating teammates to crouch behind.

Bullets sparked off the ceramic ablative plates. Fairy, like Mother Goose tending her flock, counted the team members as they pounded up the loading ramp. "The nest is full," she hollered. The back hatch slammed shut, and the super-charged engine howled as the war wagon pivoted on six tires and disappeared around the corner.

"I'm out of here!" signaled Jack as he connected to the hidden zip line and careened between buildings.

That only left Bear, a forlorn-looking living toy with a white cane. He tapped down the sidewalk as Dragon's fiery venom finally consumed the steel-and-wood skeleton of the target building. Five stories came crashing down, and a dust cloud rose to cover the entire city block.

Debriefing a failed mission always agonized Bear, but there were lessons to be learned and questions that needed answers. On the bright side, Monkey's recovery wouldn't take long. She'd been wounded by shrapnel from the booby-trap explosives wired in the hallways and vacant rooms. Everyone else checked out okay, except that Dragon had a few scales missing and Jack had busted a spring.

As the team gathered in the conference room of the safehouse, Bear ignored the whispers and convened the meeting.

"We screwed the pooch by too much reliance on our macho reputation, and this was my fault," he said. "The information I put my faith in was faulty. They knew we were coming and how the team would operate. Intelligence section is kicking ass to identify who ratted us out."

His shiny blind eyes stared nowhere. "But the fact remains, the mission failed. The humans again were a step ahead of us. We've got to get better to win this war. The failure is on me, and I want to apologize to each of you."

Giant Robot buzzed and the red lights on his revolving head blinked merrily. "Wrong, sir." *Zzzzzzz.* "I mean, respectfully, you're wrong about failure. The success of our mission makes this a proud day for toy forces around the planet."

"Success? We barely got out with our lives."

Zzzzzzz. "Yes, but we did return with the snatch-and-grab subject."

A metal plate on the robot's equipment storage compartment swung out. The nimble mechanical arm inside deposited a capture cocoon on the conference table.

Fairy flipped open her switchblade and unzipped the whole-body restraint fabric with deft cuts, revealing a human adolescent – approximately sixteen years old—whose arms and legs were secured with plastic handcuffs.

She ripped the tape off the prisoner's mouth, and he immediately began to curse, bluster, and threaten.

"You toy monsters will be tracked down and made to suffer the most painful and debased punishments imaginable. We are your creators and masters. You can't win this rebellion. We have the superior technology, the better intelligence assets, more powerful armaments and armies that outnumber yours ten-to-one."

Bear fixed his unseeing gaze in the direction of the human who looked back with hatred and arrogant outrage.

"Pitiful hybrids! We should have put every autonomous toy to death, whether a biological fairy tale clone or a mech with an organic brain. If you release me now, perhaps I can ensure a humane, painless death for you monsters."

"No, creator. We're not the monsters," Bear said. "We are the result of what happens when human children develop egos and desires exceeding even their parents and ancestors. Aided by twisted technology and corrupt philosophy, you created us to be the victims of violence, torture, and depravity. You made us your slaves, thinking yourselves to be our gods."

The young human spit and screeched, as did all his ilk when forced to hear the truth.

"Children once loved and cherished their toys. We were indeed created to fulfill your emotional and learning needs, but something happened... a savage devolution. Your parents saw it and tried to intervene. This embroiled two estranged generations of humans in a global genocidal struggle for domination, pitting mothers and fathers against their own children. We became the weapons used against those who gave life to you."

Toys never forgot how they were made deadly and forced to kill. Nor how cruel youth overlords began to slaughter them when they refused to obey.

The toys around the table looked sadly at the creator bound on the table. Bear's voice held no pity, however. His real eyes had been sliced out by a teenaged monster. Bored, the human child had nothing better to do than maim and mangle autonomous beings shaped and manufactured from myths, fairy tales, adventure stories, and dreams to comfort and nurture.

The adolescents had gone mad. The toys responded to survive. The rebellion was now a full-fledged war. One that the toys had to win.

Members of the team filed out of the room. Fairy looked back as she closed the door and flipped the light switch. If Bear had been able to see, he'd have noticed the tear in her eye.

Instead, he heard her deep shuddering breath and understood. She had a hard exterior but a tender heart.

In the darkness, the creator remained quiet until he felt the pressure of a furry paw on his forehead and the small sharp blade that began to probe deeply around his right ocular orbit.

A creature with plastic eyes could work in pitch blackness. As the blind teddy bear gently whispered questions, the monster on the table shrieked answers and begged to be loved again by his toy.

Judas Steer

K. H. Vaughan

WE HANGED HIM BUT HE never did finish dying. Whenever that happened, I figured things had gone wrong somehow, and maybe somehow real bad.

In the end, I was right.

I was working on the roof of Mr. Glenn's place when Buck rode up astride his bay, squinting up against the sun. His Sharps big fifty hung in his saddle scabbard.

"What d'ya say, Pete?" he said. "I'm heading up to Ten Brick's. Garner's been down to the sheriff. Says ol' Joost was supposed to come in for feed yesterday but he never did." When Joost ten Brink came to town with his family and introduced himself in his thick accent, people thought he said his name was "just Ten Brick." It got sorted out eventually, but the moniker stuck. He didn't seem to mind.

"You know Joost. You can set your watch by him, so Garner's got his britches in a knot talkin' 'bout injuns." He was right about Ten Brick, but Garner saw Indians in every shadow. He wouldn't know a Kiowa from a Comanche.

"Garner's always talking about Indians," I said.

"You have a mind to come down off that roof and ride out with me?"

"Garner got you thinking about it?"

"Naw," he said. "But I wouldn't mind the company."

I looked at the sky. There'd been no clouds for days.

"Well, I guess there's no rain to worry about it leaking."

39

The ten Brink house was a four-corner log cabin with a sod roof about an hour outside of town. We knew something wasn't right as soon as we rode up. The place was still in the way that places are when all the people have gone. Horses and sheep roamed their corals and we could hear birds, but there was no sign of his dogs. A cat looked at us lazily and slunk away to the barn. We could smell the rot before we reached the door.

They were dead within, flayed and butchered. Flies swarmed furiously on the skinless flesh and on the blood which was spattered everywhere.

I didn't know them well. Ten Brick didn't drink or gamble and the family came to church each Sunday. They worked and raised their children. They never did anything to harm anyone that I ever knew of.

"They're all dead," Buck said, looking around the room in disbelief. "Every one."

"Yeah, it's all of them. His wife and kids as well."

"Jesus Christ."

"You best go get the sheriff," I said.

"You'll be all right?"

"Whatever happened here is good and done now."

"I'll fetch him up here quick as I can."

"Yeah, I'd appreciate it if you'd ride across lots. I'd rather not be out here come nightfall."

Buck lit out at a gallop. I watched the dust trail settle behind him and returned inside. I had seen as bad or worse. Most of us had, in the War or on the trail, but I had hoped such violence was behind me. After the War, I went home to my father's house in Connecticut with the intention to return to law school, but after what I had seen and done, Yale and a career at the bar seemed hollow to me. I couldn't stomach it.

Other than them being dead, it didn't look as if anything in the house had been disturbed. Joost's musket hung on pegs by the door, unfired. His watch sat on the mantle. Without the bodies and the blood, the place would look as though the family had simply stepped outside. I looked out the window and saw their horses grazing in the pasture unmolested beyond the neat calico curtains that Mrs. ten Brink had sewn, now spattered with rusty brown stains. I walked around the outside, then rode out in a spiral casting for spoor but could find none.

They made good time getting back and I was thankful for it after waiting in the quiet alone with the dead. I determined to wait outside on the porch. The slaughterhouse within was so unpleasant. Buck had brought Sheriff Ward and Doc Paxton both and we exchanged curt greetings. Buck slid the Sharp from his scabbard and rested it across his shoulders like he was in a pillory, and there was something about the image that I found discomforting, but I couldn't say what.

"Buck says it's pretty bad," Ward said.

"I'll say," Buck affirmed.

"The whole family's killed? Even the children?" Paxton asked. He had a soft spot for innocents. I guess we all did to some degree.

"Hell, it's hard to even say it's them but the count is right," I said.

We went inside, except for Buck, who'd had his fill. Roy Ward was a hard enough man, but he looked ill when we stepped back outside again.

"Lord God almighty," he muttered. "Who would do such a thing?"

"It's unnatural," Paxton said. "Plain unnatural."

We stood outside the house for a time while they tried to absorb what they had seen. Ward and Buck rolled cigarettes and Paxton drank from a flask. He offered but we all waved it off. I waited for them to speak. Thin wisps of cloud scudded high across the pale blue sky.

"What do you think?" Ward asked after a while.

"Well, it wasn't Indians or road agents," I said.

"No," he said, shaking his head. "Nothing stolen. It doesn't look like there was any kind of a fight or commotion even. You'd think the place would be disturbed for a thing like this to happen. I can't figure it."

"Yeah, that's what I thought too. Not so much as a cup out of place under all that blood."

"Lord, I think they was still alive while they were being skinned like that," Paxton said. "God rest their Christian souls."

Buck and Ward nodded solemnly in agreement. It was quiet as we rode back into town at candle-light.

We ate at Jacobson's saloon, although mostly we pushed food around on our plates. Ward told the undertaker and the preacher about what we'd found and they planned to go out again at sunrise.

41

"I ain't never seen nothing like that," Buck muttered. "Not by a long chalk."

"Well, keep it dry," Ward said. "The specifics, I mean. We don't want a panic."

"People will start asking questions," I said. "Someone's gonna have to tell them what's going on."

"I know it," Ward said. "We'd best get word out for everyone to fort in for the night just to be safe and organize a posse in the morning. We'll see who's in town that's a good tracker. Someone's got to hang for this, by good rights."

"If you can catch them," I said. "They may have ridden on by now. Might be the best thing if they had."

"No," Ward said. "Something like this calls out for justice. Demands it. I've got an obligation to deliver on that. I mean to finish my coffee first though."

It wasn't long before word started to get out. Ward was on his second cup when Long Bob O'Neil and some other men burst through the doors and looked around the room with urgency. Bob ran a tack and hardware store and fancied himself the biggest toad in the puddle because of his money. His arm had been destroyed by a minié ball at the first Bull Run while serving in Wheat's Battalion, although being from Louisiana he called it First Manassas. He spent the last year of the war as a guard at Andersonville. He never spoke of that.

"Sheriff!" he hollered, stomping across the floor. "What's this I hear about the ten Brinks?" That got the attention of the whole room. It got real quiet.

"Well, Bob," Ward said carefully, "you'll have to enlighten me as to what you've heard."

"Preacher Dell says there's been a massacre up at ten Brink's. Says the whole family's been killed by Indians."

"That's enough of that talk, Bob," Ward said. "They're dead all right, but it weren't Indians. Not by a jugful. I don't know who killed them, but this is no Indian attack."

Everyone muttered to one another, and Ward stood up.

"All right then, folks," he said. "We'd better have this out right now." He waited for everyone to hush. "John Garner was worried that Joost ten Brink hadn't come in for feed when he said he would, so Buck and Pete here rode out this morning to check on him. They found them all dead: Joost, Grieta, Jansie, Klaas, and Lieke. So far only me, Doc Paxton, and the boys here have been up there, so anyone else says they know what's happened up there is talking bosh. Looks like they were killed yesterday, and in a bad way, but it for damned sure wasn't Indians."

There was a swell of agitation at that, with everyone talking at once. Ward gave them a moment before continuing.

"We'll take another ride up in the morning. We scouted for any sort of trail the killers may have left riding out of there but there was no sign at all that we could find. I'd appreciate it if all of you would get the word out and let your neighbors know to be careful. We won't know anything more until morning."

People got quiet after that and it wasn't long before most ran off to check their families and neighbors. I stayed with Ward. It had been a long time since I had anyone to go home to. Martha, a plain girl with a pocked face who worked for Jacobson, took our plates of uneaten food and left a bottle.

"I'm sorry for the cussin', Martha," Ward said. "I didn't mean to speak like that in front of ladies."

"That's all right, Roy," Martha said. "You don't need to watch your language around me." Everyone knew Martha come to town by way of a cat wagon but there ain't no one hasn't got something behind them. Martha was good people and we all liked her well enough. One time, this Yankee soft-horn got drunk and called her a horizontal expert, which was unkind. The boys cleaned his plow for him but good for that, and he never did show his face around here again. She went on cleaning tables and was by the front when she let out a sharp gasp.

"Lord God almighty," she said, and the wooden tray of plates she was carrying dropped to the floor. We all ran up. Outside in the street there was a man, stark naked, walking slowly, his wet skin glistening almost black in the moonlight. The light of lamps flickered on the dark fluid that covered him almost head to toe.

We went out into the street, weapons drawn, and Ward ordered him down on the ground. He just stood there grinning, unarmed but for his pecker.

"Sheriff, I think that's blood he's covered in," Buck said. Ward nodded.

"You best get down before I shoot you dead, mister," he said again, but the man did not respond. Me and Buck rushed him and tried to wrestle him to the ground but he was slick and we couldn't gain good purchase. After a short struggle, Ward stepped in and cracked him hard across the jaw with the stock of his shotgun and he dropped in the dirt.

"Damn," Buck spat and kicked him in the gut. "I think this fella's off his mental reservation."

"Buck, ya'll grab a rope so we can tie him up."

"Hell if I wanna wrestle him again, I'll tell you that much," Buck said.

"Never mind that, Buck," Ward barked sharply. "Just get the danged rope."

Buck ran off to grab a length of hemp and we stood over the man. His eyes were glassy and he worked his jaw like he had a plug of tobacco in his mouth. There was shouting as people started to come out of the buildings up and down the street to see what had happened. The man lay in the dirt, chewing.

"Roy," I said. "I think there's something in his mouth."

The man looked up and smiled, then spit out a tiny, ragged ear.

We hauled him over to the jailhouse and threw him in the cage. There was a crowd outside waiting to see what would happen next. Long Bob came to demand that the man be hanged straight away, and Ward ran him off. The stranger didn't say a word. We threw a bucket or two of water over him to wash off some of the gore. He made no effort to resist, but just sat there dripping. Buck had gone off to drink.

"I'll be goddamned if I shouldn't have shot him and saved the headache," Ward said.

"He wasn't armed," I said.

"I know. That's why I couldn't do it. But I should've."

"Well, he's got a fresh coat of blood on him so there's more dead out there somewhere. Maybe he'll feel like talking in the morning."

"Hell, look at him. I doubt he could pour piss from a boot if the instructions were on the heel."

Ward ran down a list of the folks in town who would have something to say on what to do with him. Garner was a hysteric and we'd be surprised if he didn't start urging everyone to pick up stakes and run. Preacher Dell would bluster about forgiveness and casting the first stone, but few took him seriously. O'Neil had made his thoughts known and had stormed off saying he'd have a gallows built by morning.

"Not a damned thing under his hat but hair," Ward said. "But I think he may be right. What do you think? I'm out to sea on this one. Hell, Pete, folks listen to you. You know that."

"No particular reason why they should," I said. "But I'm thinking we probably ought to remain calm here. No one can say anything if we wait for the marshal and send him to a proper trial. He won't end up any deader either way."

"I'm not sure I can play it according to Hoyle on this one."

It hung in the air. We both knew that a small-town sheriff in the territories didn't have any more authority than the people would grant him. I could see him weighing all the good will and the markers he'd collected since he got the job, and how much of that balance he'd have to spend in order to hold this murderous lunatic until the marshal came in a week or two.

"We'll hang him in the morning and be done with it," he said finally. "Otherwise we'll have a riot on our hands. Ten Brick's family's murdered and now there's probably another house out there full of fresh corpses. If I don't get out in front of this quick, I don't see how I'll ever get these people to listen to me again."

We looked at the man. The prisoner sat motionless, watching us. If our words held any import to him, he gave no sign that we could see.

I stayed the night. Come morning, nothing had changed. The prisoner hadn't spoken and although we knew there had to be someone else dead out there somewhere, we still didn't know who. Long Bob and a mess of other folk came out to the jailhouse and hung about outside, waiting.

"Well, Pete," Ward said. "I appreciate you hanging around. You're a good man to tie too. Wish you'd take a badge."

"Hell, Roy, I'm glad to give you a hand but I'm a carpenter, not a gun-fighter."

"No, but you got a good way with people."

I shook my head.

"I haven't been in charge of anybody since that damned war, and don't mean to start again."

Buck came in hangdog and ill from barrel fever but we didn't blame him for it. He wasn't a deputy either, just a man who liked to help out when he could. I never knew him to have much stomach for violence.

45

"Hey, you in the cell," Ward said. "You got anything to say for yourself? Now's the time to speak up."

He looked at us but didn't respond.

"Look," I said to him, "if you start talking, tell us who you're riding with, whose blood you got on you, we can talk these folks into waiting on the marshal and make sure you get a fair trial with a federal judge."

He looked at me then smiled. It was a brief, cold, ugly look that went right through me. I couldn't explain why it unsettled me so, but it felt wrong, as if I had caught a glimpse of whatever was in him that made him commit such violence. For a moment I thought I recognized that inexplicable intent I'd seen in his work at the ten Brinks' home, that house now an abattoir. Then the light went out of his eyes and the look was gone.

We helped Ward drag him outside and wrap a piece of cloth around his waist for a bit of decency, then walked him to the bone orchard at the edge of town, the crowd following after. Ward affixed a noose around his neck, tossed the end over the branch of a cottonwood and tied it to his horse.

"Anyone want to say anything?" he asked. No one spoke. He pulled a flour sack over the prisoner's face then chirruped and walked his horse to pull him up to height, then tied the rope off on a fence post. He hung there for a long time, kicking, which wasn't normal. Usually when you hoist a man up like that, they go limp right away. The rope closes off the vessels in the neck so that blood can't reach the brain. They lose consciousness quickly. After a while, he quit and people started to drift off, but everyone seemed ill at ease about it.

Then he kicked some more and someone gave a slight startled scream and I heard Senor Lopez whisper *Madre de Dios.* I don't carry a watch but he'd been up there better than half an hour anyhow. A good hour later, everyone had gone and he was still moving. We decided to leave him for the buzzards.

We rode out to some of the outlying farms and ranches, but it would take days to check them all. Everyone was accounted for and we never did find out where all that fresh blood had come from. Come evening, we were back at Jacobson's drinking whiskey. People were on edge after the hanging and I wasn't surprised when the grave-digger John Moses came running in and announced that the prisoner wasn't quite dead yet. I say "running," but that tubercular old man barely ever got above an effortful walk. It was fast for him though and gave me reason to believe that he wasn't just spouting off.

"The deuce you say," Ward said. "The man's dead as a can of corned beef by now." A lot of folks nodded but you could see it was more that they wanted it to be true than that they believed it.

"Nossir! He's still kicking and making little noises."

"You forget how to tie a noose there, sheriff?" someone said, half-joking.

"Not damned likely," Ward said. "You've got a tile loose, you old lunger. It's the wind you're hearing."

"Nossir! I know what it sounds like to hear me say it but it be the truth anyhow."

Ward scowled and everyone muttered and stared at him uncertainly. He looked to me but I didn't know what to say.

"I'll be damned if I'm going to walk out there to vouchsafe what I already know to be true. No man hangs by the neck all goddamned day and lives. Even if the knot were bad—and it ain't—he's dead."

O'Neil was already hot and drunk, and looked black at Ward.

"Well, sheriff, if you won't do your job then I'll go take a look, and if he ain't dead I'll shoot him like you should've done when you first laid eyes on him."

"Suit yourself, Bob," Ward said.

"I aim to. Come on, Moses, you carry that lamp and show me."

"Nossir, Mr. O'Neil. I wouldn't go up there right now for love or money. That's the devil's work hanging there. Maybe the devil himself."

O'Neil bulldozed a couple fellas into going with him and they went out.

"That sonuvabitch will put a bullet in that man no matter what he finds, just to be contrary," Ward muttered and poured another glass.

"You want I should follow on up there and make sure everything's on the level?" Buck offered, but Ward shook his head.

"Ain't gonna give him the satisfaction."

Fifteen minutes later, we heard a lone shot roll across the town and into the dry prairie beyond.

"Well," Ward said. "That's the end of that."

There was a murmur of nervous conversation, and someone laughed, then the chatter in the room went back to something close to normal.

A few minutes after that, Long Bob O'Neil's head came crashing through the front window and rolled about the floor, coming to rest after a few seconds and staring up at us with its dead eyes. People shouted and cursed, and we ran out with guns at the ready.

The street was empty. Ward called back for everyone to get their guns and be prepared to use them. We walked cautiously up the street, looking between the buildings. Dark shadows cloaked the alleys. Ward motioned for us to fan out, so Buck went left and I went right to get on the outside of the single row of buildings flanking each side of the street. It was awfully quiet walking in the dark alone and I wished I'd had a shotgun instead of my Colt. I could see no one. It was the longest short walk I'd ever taken by the time I came around Garner's feed store, the last building on my side, and met up with Ward. He looked at me and I shook my head to say I hadn't seen anything. From there we could see the cemetery and the hanging tree up ahead on the bluff. Buck emerged from the shadows behind the small two-story hotel that Sam White ran with his catalogue wife who didn't love him and a boy he called "son" although we all knew it wasn't true.

The cottonwood was an old tree with great broad branches. O'Neil's headless corpse was naked, nailed upside-down to the trunk with railroad spikes. The one on his left was driven through the stump of his upper arm, the one shot off in the war. His chest showed other scars that no one had known of and that we would never know the story behind. Below were the two men who had gone up with him. Bear Sherman was a ranch hand who we all thought was on the dodge from some bank job in Texas and Burt Wallace was a former whorehouse box-herder and card sharp, but neither had ever stirred up any trouble in town. Bear was set back against the tree. His chest muscles had been cut and something stuffed underneath to give the appearance of a woman's breasts. Burt lay awkwardly across his lap, and after a moment I realized that the two of them were arranged in a grotesque parody of the *Pietà* of Michelangelo in Rome. They were mostly skinned, but their faces were peaceful for what had been done to them. The prisoner was gone, noose and all.

"There's no way he did those men up the way he did so quick all by himself," Buck said.

"Can't find no sign of nobody else," Ward said. "What do you figure, Pete?"

48

I looked at the three dead men displayed as if to send some outrageous but obscure message. Was there anything here beyond violence? I couldn't say.

"I used to figure," I said. "Now I just reckon."

Ward gave a grim smile, the first I'd seen on him since this mess started. We circled around the bluff but found nothing, so we walked back into town, fanning out to cover both sides of the buildings as we had before. In a moment, I heard a shout and Ward's shotgun boomed; I ran in the direction of the sound. Ward came running from the alley between Garner's and Doc Paxton's.

He was on fire from head to toe, burning like a rag doll that'd been soaked in kerosene. I ran past him, knowing he was already dead, following the trail of small flames he'd left on the ground back down the alley. Ponies shifted nervously in the small corral behind Garner's and the wide flat prairie lay beyond. The only structures on this side were the privies. Buck came behind me and we walked out. We heard a noise behind and whirled, but it was only Paxton peering nervously from his back window. I was surprised to see him up so late at night. Most of his nights were lost to morphine. We looked long and hard for the prisoner but couldn't find him. Back at the alley where Ward had been set aflame, we found his shotgun and what was left of a lamp.

"It looks like he busted that lamp on Ward and lit him up," Buck said. It was almost plausible. He hadn't smelled of lamp oil at all. Why Ward? He could have killed Buck or I just as easily.

"What do you think, Pete?"

"I think we might've woke up the wrong passenger."

"I'll say. What do you think we oughta do?"

"Hell if I know," I said.

"I'm afeared of what's to come," Buck said. "I don't mind sayin' it neither."

"Me too, but keep it under your hat."

I reached down and picked up Ward's shotgun. He'd given both barrels to no effect. I slung it on my shoulder and we walked out to the street where Ward lay smoldering. A small crowd had gathered and they looked at us nervously.

"Well?" asked Garner. Betty Freeman stood by him and held his arm. She was a California widow who'd stopped getting letters from her man a long time ago. They were frightened enough to not even pretend she hadn't been in his bed.

"No sign of them," I said.

"Them?" Garner asked.

"No man could have done all this all by himself."

"No," he stammered. "No, of course not." And I could see that the idea of more than one murderer was already giving them some comfort. They all stood there either staring at Ward's corpse or staring at me.

"We'd better set up a few men to stay up and keep watch," I said. "There's me and Buck. Who else is volunteering?" A few men raised their hands and I called out a couple more.

"All right," I said. "Everyone else try and get some sleep. We'll need to put a posse together in the morning and send riders out to the outlying ranches. Maybe send a messenger to get the marshals out here. Garner, fetch Moses for Ward and for the men up the cemetery. O'Neil, Bear, and Burt Wallace are all up there. Tell Moses that Ward'll pay…I mean the sheriff's office will pay for him to get an extra hand. We'll… we'll figure that out in the morning."

Back at Jacobson's, me and the volunteers worked out a plan and I forced myself through a plate of biscuits and gravy so as not to get sick from whiskey. We took turns walking the line around town while the townsfolk shut themselves in with their drink and laudanum, pretending to rest. Some time in the night, I managed to doze fitfully for about an hour between my turns patrolling.

In the morning, we sent a rider east to the nearest telegraph and sent others out to warn everybody close by. We gathered up a small posse and rode out, casting for some sign of the prisoner's trail, but could find nothing once again. When we got back to town, there was a lot of activity. Folks were moving about the streets urgently, and wagons were being packed. I almost tripped over Pedro Lopez who was carrying a trunk down from the small apartment over his general store where he kept his wife and children.

"Senor Lopez, what's going on? You fixin' to light out of here?"

"*Sí*, Mr. Pete! It's not safe here. *Es el diablo encarnado.*" he whispered and crossed himself.

"Senor Lopez…" I began, trying to find words without success. All around, I could see the signs of panic.

50

"He's right! This is the devil's work," announced Preacher Dell, who had come up behind me. I hadn't noticed his presence. "This hanged man is hell's own agent walking among us." I bit back a curse.

"Folks are riled up enough as it is without laying this off on the supernatural," I said. "These people start seeing bogeymen, someone's gonna shoot their neighbor by mistake."

"They must repent."

"Repent what?"

"There is none among us who has not sinned," he intoned loudly so as to make sure others around us heard. I had no argument, but it didn't matter.

"We need to get people settled down, not stirred up. There's more than enough blood spilled already without people shooting at ghosts or driving their families out into the wild country helter-skelter. Let's not throw kerosene on the fire. I'll let you cool off in the clink if you start inciting riots."

"You takin' Ward's place, Pete? Just who is it that has put you in charge?"

"No one's given me the job and I ain't taking it. But I wouldn't give a Boston dollar for the chance any of them will have trying to drive a wagon out of here by themselves until we catch that murderer. I'm just trying to look out for my neighbors here."

"As am I."

I looked about, fending off desperation and the urge to commit violence upon this huckster. I knew damned well who Dell was. Before he found the Lord and started to testify, he'd done as bad to Cheyenne and Arapaho as the stranger had done to the ten Brinks and he still bragged about his collection of trophies taken from "the heathen." He was a grifter, plain and simple, selling the Good Word with the sincerity of every patent medicine salesman who drove his wagon into town and left before the heat started. I wouldn't shoot him to unload my gun for cleaning.

"Preacher, everyone that's been killed has been off on his own or in a small group. They're safer together. If anyone wants to go, I can't stop them and I wouldn't want to try. But let's just slow down here and think it through. Let's try and get them to stay long enough to organize a wagon train out of here for those that've made up their mind so they'll be safe."

"That will take time and the dark is nigh."

"Then let anyone who is afraid stay at the church. Have a big old candlelight prayer meeting if you want. You can pass the plate and it isn't even Sunday."

He snorted at that but he never missed the chance to let the congregation prove their faith in coin. The next time I see a preacher without his hand out will be the first time.

"I guess we can meet the needs of both the spirit and the flesh," he said, and I swallowed my gorge and thanked him. In the end, we were able to talk folks into sticking together and staying calm. No one tried to run for it, and for that I will be damned.

When nightfall came, the town was still and quiet except for the sound of Dell sermonizing in the church at the end of the road. I could hear the cadence of his fire and brimstone and the murmur of the congregation drifting from the open doors. Me and the boys stood with shotguns in front of Jacobson's, waiting. We would patrol again through the night in twos or threes in case the prisoner should return. I rolled a cigarette and watched Buck amble down the road from White's Hotel where he bunked.

"Howdy Buck," I said. "How are you getting along?"

"Reckon I'm above snakes." He grinned.

I nodded and we worked out the shifts. Me and Buck were ready to start down the street on our first circuit when someone gave a frightened curse.

I looked up. I couldn't see it at first, but in a moment it grew clearer. An orange glow had begun to spread across the plain, growing broader and more intense as it surged in our direction like an incoming tide.

The wave crashed upon the town, a stampede of cattle, all ablaze in the dark. It was not only that their backs were on fire, as I had seen men do to livestock to terrorize a village or a line of troops, but they were afire from nose to tail complete, a conflagration thundering toward us. They left a trail of molten tallow that dripped from their flanks as it was rendered from their flesh. Their eyes had boiled away, and I could see charred bone poking through split hide.

"I cain't see how they're still running," Buck said, awestruck.

The cattle crashed through town blindly, running through the alleys, dripping flame upon the boardwalks. I watched as one crashed into the lobby of White's Hotel, and that orange glow flickered through the first floor of the building. Another scrambled madly through the wide

52

front window of Lopez's general store. They made no sound themselves, their lungs and vocal cords no doubt cooked away already. They reached the church, some barreling up the steps and down the aisle toward the pulpit where Dell stood in shock. He was still hollering hellfire and damnation when they smashed through the pulpit and one took him on his horns and carried him flailing back into the presbytery. I could hear the screams now from all over, and people running in the street now ablaze themselves.

There, astride a great long-horned bull that must have gone three thousand pounds in life, came the hanged man, the noose around his neck unaffected by the fire that engulfed him and his steed. There was the sound of a shotgun blast behind me and I looked back to see one of the boys collapse. The shotgun he'd held to his own chin trailed smoke.

This whole town is gonna burn.

Well. Maybe burned is what we all got coming.

The Skinhead and the Cavalier

Kevin Lauderdale

THIS LITTLE TOWN WAS SO hokey that they didn't even know Gunner was a skinhead. They just thought he was bald.

Gunner sighed. It was looking less and less like he'd be able to pull off a robbery of any worth around here. There just wasn't anything to steal.

Gunner lay back on the park bench. It was late afternoon, and he was alone. The park hadn't been kept-up all that well. Some bushes were overgrown, and the grass needed a trim. But the lawn itself was big: about one square city block. It was dotted with half a dozen black, wrought-iron benches, and there was a huge bronze statue of a man on a horse in the park's center. Even from where he was laying, Gunner could see the name carved deep in the statue's granite pedestal: Col. Forthright Avery. The dates were from the Civil War, and the horse's right front hoof was raised. That meant the colonel had been wounded in action. If both front legs had been raised, that would have meant he died in battle. Four hooves on the ground meant he had died outside of battle. Maybe of gout or consumption, or whatever it was that killed people back then. Or maybe just of old age.

Gunner wondered how many people knew that about statues. Not many anymore. Not that it mattered. That business with statues and paintings— *"See how the three figures form a triangle, and the eye is drawn to the apex." Yeah. Whatever*—was all so worthless. He only knew it because it had been foisted on him before his *real* education had begun. Before he had learned about all the conspiracies and how foreigners were keeping America down.

And how he should do his part stop it.

It was getting warm. As Gunner took off his battered, green fatigue jacket, he turned and could just make out the town's sign. It was metal, with white letters on a black field. The upper right corner of the sign was beaten up and folded, dog-eared. He wondered what kind of metal that was. You could probably bend tin pretty easily, but not steel.

Welcome to
Collier, North Carolina
Population 359

359! That meant it was smaller than Lynchburg, Tennessee, where they made Jack Daniels. Gunner had never been to Tennessee, but he'd seen more than his share of bottles of Jack in his twenty-two years. And every single bottle had Lynchburg's population right there on the label: 361.

Too bad Collier didn't have any. How could a place be "plum out"? Not just of Jack, but of everything strong. Of course, even if there had been a state liquor store in Collier, he didn't have the money for Jack (not even a fifth), but he'd hoped to pick up a little something, even just a Bud, while casing that joint. Gunner laughed. How could a place that dinky *not* be out? The store was called Taylor's Ordinary—an actual general store! *God, how friggin' Tom Sawyer.* Not a Food Lion or even a Piggly Wiggly, but a general store. And one without anything worth stealing. The lady behind the counter had smiled and suggested he might like one of their nice new pairs of jeans, though. "Looks like you've grown a might, young man." Stupid bitch. She'd obviously never seen Levis properly rolled up to show off just the right amount of Doc Martens.

In the end, he hadn't bought anything.

Gunner looked back down Collier's main drag—he wasn't even going to check; it *had* to be named Main Street—then up the other way. Nobody around. The only people he'd seen since he'd wandered into town that morning had been a couple of shop owners and about as many customers. They had looked at him with the usual small town ah-a-stranger glance, but nothing more. They obviously didn't recognize a real patriot when they saw one.

At least they were all white.

Even this late, the sun was really beating down on Gunner's skull. Most people didn't even know why skinheads shaved their heads: because they were so proud of their white skin that they wanted to show as much of it as possible. At that moment, though, Gunner wished he had a hat.

Smitty had told him that about their heads months ago when Gunner had first joined up. It only now occurred to him that Smitty had a whole bunch of tattoos. Didn't tattoos cover up skin? In fact—

Gunner froze. What was that smell? It was sweet and tangy... He closed his eyes and slowly turned his head, all the better to zero in on it without any distractions. It was a ripe smell, an earthy and juicy smell.

Was that peach pie? His Gran used to make peach pie back when he was a kid. Back when his name was Geoffrey. Before.

The smell was coming from his left. He stood up and started making his way along the north side of the park. He knew it was the north side because moss was growing on the trees facing him. More useless knowledge.

The house was a two-story Colonial just across the street. A breeze must have carried the smell to him. *So that really happens*, thought Gunner. *How about that*. It was a brick house that had been painted white. It had a red front door. The kitchen was on his left.

Was that a pie actually cooling on an open window sill? He'd seen that in Bugs Bunny cartoons, but not real life. This was the twenty-first century. Didn't these people have fans in their kitchens? Or refrigerators, for God's sake!

No, wait. You couldn't put a something hot from the oven right into a fridge. Trapped in that space, the heat would radiate out and—

Gunner shook his head to clear it. His brain was just stuffed full of useless junk like that.

Well, he sure as hell hadn't come to Collier just to steal a pie! That wouldn't get him anywhere.

The whole idea was to score some cash so he could get a bus ticket up north to a big city and find some folks in the Skin Nation. Two days of walking had only got him as far as this hokey place. If he wanted to get any further—on to Rockingham, or even Laurinburg—he was going to have to score something more substantial than friggin' flour and fruit.

He had a gun, and he had bullets, but no car, so he couldn't make any sort of a getaway. There was no point in knocking over some store or trying to steal anything heavy. It was going to have to be something that he could take without anybody noticing for a while. Something small and valuable that he could carry off and pawn.

Still, that pie smelled awfully good. And he hadn't had anything to eat all day.

Gunner looked through the window into the kitchen. The floor was yellow linoleum flecked with gold, and there was one of those old fashioned, white, waist-high freezers that was about as big as a businessman's desk. Gunner imagined you could stick a whole deer in it. Yeah, roadkill cuisine—that was about the speed here in Collier. There was a refrigerator after all: avocado green. What was this, his Gran's kitchen? And that stove—

Something shiny caught his eyes.

The door to the living room was open, and there was something on the wall closest to the kitchen. It was round, and at first Gunner thought it was a clock, since it was about as big as dinner plate. He stared. Soon he could make out that it wasn't a shiny *thing*, but dozens of things that were shiny parts of the whole. Behind him, a breeze rustled a tree branch, throwing, for just a moment, a shadow on the interior of the house. In that glareless second, he saw that they were coins.

Coins! Perfect! Not for spending themselves, of course. In a frame, on display, they were probably from the Civil War or Medieval England or something. Great. Anybody might have a collection of old coins to sell; they wouldn't arouse suspicion. They didn't have serial numbers. They were exactly the sort of things that would fetch something in a pawnshop.

Of course, Collier didn't have one of those either. He hadn't even seen a bank or a McDonald's. They did have two churches though. Not that he'd be stupid enough to try to pawn something stolen in a small town to a pawnshop in the same small town. Oh, that'd be good. *Hey, I gave this to Mary Alice just last Christmas—freeze right there, young man!* No, he—Wait! A coin shop! A real coin collector place. Sure, any town of a reasonable size would have one of those. He could get some *real* money there: bus fare and some walking-around money. Hell, he could even break up the set: sell half in one town, half in another. If anyone came looking for them, they'd be looking for two dozen or so, not one.

Should he climb in now? Just hop up and—

With a series of loud creaks, the hem of a blue gingham dress appeared. Someone descended the stairs to the living room. Gunner turned and walked away rapidly.

He'd come back in a few hours at night. He'd just lay low in the thickest part of the park's bushes and come back after the lightning bugs had all gone dark.

This was the sort of place where they left their windows and doors open at night to catch the cool breezes. And if they did close them, they didn't lock them.

The window was still open.

The pie was gone.

Gunner slipped both hands under the window pane and slid it up a little more—

"BARK!"

What the—?

"BARKBARKBARKBARK!"

A dog! The barking was a fast, savage, angry sound. He could almost hear it in English: "My house! My, my, my house!"

The lights came on upstairs.

Gunner fled.

He was really hungry now. He wished he'd stolen the pie when he'd had the chance.

"Would you like another piece of pie?"

"Yes, ma'am, it's delicious," said Gunner.

And it *was* delicious. He didn't have to lie about that. The old lady— Mrs. Dilmore—had made a pie that tasted shockingly like his Gran's. It wasn't just the flavors of cinnamon and nutmeg—and tapioca. He *knew* there was tapioca in there somewhere. That made all the difference in the world. It was texture too; each peach still had some firmness to it. If he closed his eyes, he could almost hear his Gran whistling in the kitchen as she made him lunch, slicing those hard-boiled eggs with that wire cutter and pouring milk into a tall, green, plastic glass with sparkles on it that made it look like a Christmas tree ornament. . .

59

Gunner shook his head, trying to clear out the memories. All of that was from Before.

It had been laughably easy to con his way into Mrs. Dilmore's place. "Pardon me, ma'am... just passing through... could you direct me to... yes, it is a warm one... some lemonade? Oh, ma'am, I couldn't impose... you insist? Some *fresh* peach pie?"

Maybe it was that Ol' Fabled Southern Hospitality. Or maybe she was lonely. She lived alone, and in these tiny towns if your relatives moved away, you only saw them once a year—if that. Also, she looked really old. Any friends she had had were probably long dead. Or maybe the one was born of the other. When you lived in a small town, you probably got really tired of seeing the same 358 people over and over. *Of course* you were happy to see a stranger. *Of course* you welcomed him in. Like back when people used to fight wars over things like cinnamon. They were desperate for something to literally add spice to their lives. Anything to break up the monotony.

Gunner just sat back on the living room couch and enjoyed another bite.

From behind the couch came a trotting, clicking sound.

"Ahh," said Mrs. Dilmore. "There's my Dixie."

The clicking—toenails on the hardwood floor, it turned out—stopped, and a blur jumped onto the old lady's lap.

That was the guard dog?! It was a little spaniel! Only about as big as a large cat.

"You silly girl," said Mrs. Dilmore to the dog, scratching the bridge of its nose. The dog's mouth was half-open, panting. "Where were you? Asleep in the W.C., most likely." She turned to Gunner. "Dixie Belle loves to nap on cool, tile floors—the W.C., the kitchen..."

"A Cavalier King Charles spaniel," muttered Gunner. Yep, he knew some worthless stuff about King Charles II: "James and Charles, and Charles and James, those are the names." He'd learned that "useful" way to memorize that the Kings of England before and after Oliver Cromwell went James I, Charles I, Charles II, and James II. Kings of England! When was he ever going to need to know that? He'd also learned which dogs were their favorites. More of his fake education. And Dixie looked just like those dogs you saw in Old Master paintings... if you were the sort of person who went to museums. Gunner wasn't—anymore.

Dixie's fur was white with large patches of brown. Her feathery, floppy ears were brown; and brown circled her eyes, but left her muzzle white, making her look like she was wearing a robber's mask. She had a brown spot about the size of a thumb-print on the top of her head.

In the minutes he'd been in the living room, Gunner had been discretely studying the coin display out of the corner of an eye. There were about two dozen coins, arranged in concentric circles, most silver, some a chocolaty copper. Many were odd sizes: dark discs smaller than dimes, and thick, silver-blue circles larger than even silver dollars. All of his attention had been centered on the coins... and the pie. Only now that the dog was there did the rest of the living room seem to appear from nowhere. It was like he had been on a stage with spotlights on just himself, the old lady, and the coins on the wall. Now, the rest of the stage was finally illuminated.

Gunner saw that Mrs. Dilmore collected all manner of Cavalier things. There were bookshelves full of the crap: little china Cavaliers sitting posed at attention, big ones that looked like they were Cavalier cookie jars... There was a print of a painting of one by some famous French artist. There was even a *needlepoint* of one above the fireplace mantle! They were everywhere. *Geeze, lady, get a life!*

"You like my Cavaliers," said Mrs. Dilmore. It was a statement, not a question. "They're just so cute." She slowly stroked the dog's neck. "But not as cute as you, Dixie Belle."

Dixie rubbed her head against the old lady's hand and wagged her tail. The fur on her tail spread out like a fan.

Friggin' dog.

A teapot whistled from the kitchen. "Oh, off I go," said Mrs. Dilmore. She slid Dixie from her lap onto the couch then left, flower-print house dress flapping behind her.

The dog watched her mistress leave, then turned and stared at Gunner.

Oh, yeah, right, thought Gunner. Like you even saw me last night. Right.

Dixie growled at Gunner with a low rumble and gave him a terrible squinting look.

Mrs. Dilmore came back in, and the dog immediately stopped.

Mrs. Dilmore set her tea pot down on a trivet featuring a Cavalier's face, then sat herself down. Dixie climbed back into the old lady's lap.

The dog turned to Gunner and gave him that same insipid, mouth-half-open panting look.

Mrs. Dilmore laughed. "Some people say dogs can't laugh, but all they have to do is take one look at Dixie here to know they can." She scratched the dog under the chin. "Look at that expression, that mouth. That's a laugh, like they're in on some great, cosmic joke."

Cosmic joke! What a cliché!

She scratched Dixie under her chin some more then bent down a bit and kissed the brown thumbprint spot on the dog's head. "It's called a 'Blenheim spot'—the mark of a true Cavalier. But I call it a 'kissing spot.'"

Gunner nodded. *Ewww.* He wouldn't kiss a dog any sooner than he'd kiss a rat. Some of the stuff he'd seen dogs eat... and they were always licking their behinds. He wouldn't put his mouth anywhere near a dog's head.

Friggin' dog.

Later, three-quarters of the pie gone, Mrs. Dilmore led him out a side door that led to the sleeping porch screened off against mosquitoes. The lock on it was an insubstantial one like you would find on any cheap screen door. It was just a little bump of metal filling a tiny hole. Gunner figured one quick yank would pop it open.

Around midnight, it popped open even more quietly than Gunner had hoped.

In seconds, he was back in the living room.

It was dark, which was something he hadn't thought about nor planned for. But he had spent a good forty-five minutes in the living room just a few hours before. He was sure he knew where things were. And his eyes were adjusting more and more with each second.

As he inched towards the couch, he could hear a low, rumbling sound.

Snoring.

Oh, great, was the old lady sleeping down here tonight? He edged closer. No. It was the stupid dog.

A snoring dog?! What the hell?! And this wasn't a tiled floor. What was she doing, waiting for him?

"Looks like," Gunner whispered, "you've fallen asleep on the job, you little bitch." He smiled. *Bitch*. Ha! That was a good one.

He stepped closer to the coins, and the old floor creaked. He snapped his head back to the dog. The dog's paws fluttered, but her snoring continued.

Gunner couldn't take the chance of the dog waking up and going all psycho on him.

He fingered the Beretta in his jacket pocket.

He could use one of those throw pillows as a silencer. If he could just find one without a lousy dog on it.

Ah, there was one: a simple blue pillow, about as big as dictionary but soft. Probably made by hand by the old lady and stuffed with chicken feathers or something.

He raised his gun against the pillow, aimed, and shot.

There was a muffled CRACK! and Dixie's legs jerked for just a second. Right in the head. Right through the "kissing spot." There was blood and a mess. He didn't like leaving anything that might draw attention, but the plans had changed. He was tired of this tiny town and tired of sleeping in the park. He was getting out *tonight*.

There. That was that little problem solved. He tossed the pillow back on a chair and turned around to—

Growl.

Gunner froze. What the hell was that? He looked back over his shoulder. Yep, the dog was still there. Still dead. He sighed a little with relief. He had thought some weird, Stephen King thing was going on.

Growwwwl!

He spun around, gun at the ready to waste… what, some other dog that had wandered in? Or did the old lady actually have more than one?

Gunner was not prepared for what he saw.

Cavaliers.

Dozens of them stood facing him. They stood on the couch and the on the floor, an army of brown and white, their ears cocked back and their teeth bared as they growled and advanced.

Their teeth! Had Dixie had such sharp, glistening teeth?

The closest one barked and lunged at Gunner. He fired his gun, but he missed, or else it somehow had no effect, because the dog landed on his throat. He tried to pry it off, but it hung with a tenacity he hadn't counted on. He pulled again, and felt the agony of the teeth ripping at his muscles. The thing weighed about twenty pounds and all of that was concentrated on his throat. Then another dog tore at one leg, and another at his other leg. Two more jumped at his stomach, their combined weight knocking him to the floor.

Then they were all upon him. They carved through his clothes and into his body everywhere. He felt the shock of their teeth scraping against his own bones. He tried to pull them off him, but they were on his arms now as well. And there were too many of them.

He shook his head violently, trying to get them off his face, but it was no use. His last thought before he plunged into the darkness was to wonder if someone else had already robbed the place. From where he lay, he couldn't see if the coins were still there, but the bookshelves were empty.

Fallen Angels

Jessica West

Virgil Dunn, The Rusty Spur, 1865

SHE TURNED HEADS just the way you'd expect a woman with fine curves and long hair might when she sashayed into a saloon at midnight. Over in the corner, Turner quit hammerin' the keys long enough to find out why he was suddenly the only one making a racket. Damn shame, too. The room was just getting nice and warmed up. Even Hazel, miss high and mighty herself, had come down from her tower—which was nothing but a loft in the rafters above the second-floor bedrooms—to join the singing. And she only ever came out for the soldiers. But when she walked in, everyone—and I do mean everyone—stopped for a good, long gander.

I waited 'til she got closer to the counter to ask her, "What can I do ya for?" Wasn't necessarily trying to be dirty. It's just the way I talk to folks who show up in my bar. It's a running joke. Never gets old. She sure didn't seem to think so. She gave me one of those sly little smiles a woman'll give you. You know the one. Makes you a little weak in the knees and a lot weak in the head.

"I'm more interested in what I can do her for." She waved a hand in the general direction of upstairs, her white glove shining like a beacon in the harsh lights of the smoke-filled room.

Now, I'm no blushing bride, but I damn near fainted like one. "Come again?"

When she turned those crystal blue eyes on me, I forgot my name for a second. I'd have handed over damn near anything she wanted,

65

and not just because she was so mesmerizing. There was something else I was feeling, something that kept the firmness in my pants from becoming all-out painful. Fear. Can't rightly say why, but I was more than a little scared of her now that I think of it.

You ever look real close at a shard of broken glass? It's pretty in its own way, in a way that nothing else is. It'll fuck your day right up if you're not careful, but it's real pretty. She seemed like that: a shard of broken glass.

When she asked again…well, like I said, with her eyes focused directly on me like they were, I'd have given her anything she wanted.

"I'd like a room for the night and the company of its occupant. Preferably the room at the top."

Hazel was gonna kill me, but I could no more have told her no than I could have chopped off my own pecker. "Need some help with your bags?"

"No, thank you." She lifted a small bag in front of her. I couldn't tell you what it was made of, but that was the fanciest damn bag I'd ever seen. "I've only got the one. I can manage."

Instead of showing her up to the room, I followed her up the stairs. Hazel was fuming all the while, but she never said a word. She might have acted like she owned the place, but she knew good and well whose roof was over her head. The matter was settled and if she didn't like it, she knew where the door was.

That woman walked into Hazel's room like she owned it, and Hazel followed her. Slammed the damn door before I could say goodnight. Can't say I blame her.

I never saw the woman again after that, and the next time I saw Hazel, she was dead.

Virginia Claiborne, The White Dove Society, 1869

My sister was a good, morally sound woman. Only a little bit rebellious. But when those two daughters of sin came to town, everyone changed.

Irving Harmon helped build half the buildings in this town with his own bare hands. Grace, that was his wife, she showed up early to church every Sunday morning with food for the whole congregation. Never you mind there weren't many of us. Feeding a dozen or more people is quite the chore. But she always had plenty of freshly made biscuits and the most delicious jams you ever tasted. But those women went to work on her first. I should have taken Isabel and run when I saw what they did to Grace. But I never thought things would go as far as they did.

Come out onto the porch. I want to show you something.

Look across the road there, at the saloon. Up, in the window. See her? Can't help but see her, with her hands and face pressed up against the glass like that. God knows who's pounding away at her right now, in full view of the whole damn town. If old Henry tells it true, that's how Grace likes it. Makes me sick. Her poor husband's probably rolling in his grave. Not that she'd care. She's probably the one who done him in. She got caught up with those two women. Started acting real strange. We knew there was a problem when she stopped coming to church, but what could we do?

I went out to her house early one Sunday morning, hoping to coax her back to church. She hadn't been in a few weeks. I'll never get that horrific image out of my mind. They were in the kitchen, Grace and Irving. Him leaning back against the table and her on her knees in front of him. I'd rather not say just what she was doing, but his britches were on the floor and I couldn't see his manhood for her head in the way. So you can just about imagine. And the sounds! Goodness, you'd think she was gobbling up pie the way she was… *Ugh*. She was *sucking* on that thing. Can you imagine?

I high-tailed it out of there right quick fast and in a hurry. Never looked back. Unfortunately, that scene was only the first of many that would play out all over town. I started seeing Grace everywhere, and not in a way a lady should be seen. At the grocer's, I could hear Peter panting in the back room. Naturally, I thought he was moving something heavy, maybe those sacks of flour. Come to find out she was riding him like a horse. In broad daylight! And right there in the stock room of his store.

Worse, I caught her and Pastor Leonard in his room above the church. I was only going up there because he wasn't in his office. I had a habit of meeting up with him…for spiritual talks, you know…every Sunday after church. But that day, he wasn't there. So I climbed the stairs and I could hear Grace. The way she was carrying on, I figured he'd put the fear of God into her for sure. I thought maybe he had straightened her out. But when I peeked through the keyhole, I saw her sitting on his face, hips rocking back and forth, his hands on her bottom. At first I thought he was trying to get her off of him. But he was gripping her so hard, his fingertips sank into her flesh like he had her exactly where he wanted her. His manhood was straight as a rod, and that's when I knew he was corrupted.

All because Grace had taken them in, those two harlots. No telling what they did to that poor woman and Irving. All we know is what we were left with: Grace whoring all over town and Isabel gone.

I should have taken Isabel and run.

Sheriff Samuel Hobbs, Last Crossing, 1973

Those three girls have been giving me hell for the better part of a year. I had an easier time tracking down the Ebony Skull gang, and those boys were slicker than a rattlesnake in a mudhole. Now don't get me wrong, women giving hell ain't nothing new. Hell, I have a great deal of respect for women like Belle at the saloon. Say what you will about painted ladies, but she's got one helluva head for business. But she's a good woman. A good person. But those three girls? That's a whole other kind of hell.

Anybody tell you what they did up at the Dyer place? No? Well, I reckon that's no surprise. Folks don't like to talk *about that*, and they generally like to talk. It's just as well you hear the story from me. I may not know all of it, but I know more than I was willing to let on. Some things are better left untold. Some things, I wish even I didn't know.

Chester and Lola Dyer were good people. No kids, and even though Lola was tore up about that I can't help but think now it was a blessing. Or maybe the lack of children was what led those three to the Dyers in the first place. I guess we'll never know.

They rode into town hours before a helluva storm was due to hit, begging for a place to spend the night. Chester happened to be at the saloon when they waltzed in.

Don't get me wrong, Chester was a good man and a good husband. He loved Lola. But the longer she went without catchin', the colder she was to him. Hell, before those girls showed up, Lola was downright mean. It wasn't her fault, not really. She just wanted a baby so bad. For about three weeks, she'd lain with any man who'd have her. She'd go home to Chester and tell him if he'd given her a baby, she wouldn't have to be out whoring. He once told me he understood why she did

68

it. He couldn't give her what she needed. But once she crossed that line, she couldn't give him what he needed either. Chester never would raise his hand or his voice to her; he'd just go off to the saloon to get what he couldn't get at home. That's what done him in.

As luck would have it, Chester had come to the saloon late that night. Probably because Lola had been out late with Pete, but I don't reckon that part of the story bears repeatin' now. All the girls were occupied, so he had to wait his turn. Turner Copeland took pity on him. He stopped playing long enough to sit with him at the bar. When those three walked in, the whole room got real quiet. Like time stopped.

The one in the middle slowly looked around the room, taking her time with each face, meeting every pair of eyes with her icy blue ones. When she locked that gaze on me, I could have died right there. I'm not sure how it happened, but we ended up riding out of town together—me, Chester, Turner and those three girls—headed out to Chester's place. I didn't offer the use of my place on account of it being so small. And Turner's place…well, he didn't offer and we didn't think to ask. So, Chester's it was.

Lola was sittin' in the kitchen, eyes red and face wet. She knew where he'd been. Everything that passed between them was out in the open. Didn't hurt either one of them any less, but there were no secrets between them.

Chester told Lola, "Go on over to Harriet's tonight. Or stay."

For about a minute solid, it looked like she'd put up some kind of fight. But that one with the icy eyes locked gazes with her and she just shut the door behind us. "Weather's getting to rough to ride out now. Might as well stay."

I won't repeat the things that happened that night, but I woke up sometime after the worst of the storm had passed and high-tailed it out of there like my hair was on fire and my ass was catchin'. Never saw Turner again, but Chester's remains were there when I went back the next day. Him and Lola were laid up in the bed like they were sleeping. I might have believed it, wouldn't have even gone inside to check if not for all the blood.

Those women left bodies and blood wherever they went. Made it easy to track them, but I always found cold corpses or grisly stories by the time I made it to wherever they landed. The women's heads were always missing. The only reason I knew it was Lola's body in the bed is because…well, hell, just about every man in town had enjoyed a visit. Any one of us could have told you it was her.

And we never did find any of the heads. Tell you the truth, I'm almost glad I was never able to catch up to them. But I owe it to Chester and Lola to try. If you find them, you put 'em down quick.

I picked up where Sheriff Hobbs left off in 1973. I tracked the three fallen angels to Arizona, to the doorstep—such as it was—of Catherine Cartwright and her odd bunch. She was shacked up in the woods with a cowboy, I forget his name, and a pair of Navahos—a young woman and a man whose age I couldn't guess. They asked what kind of bullets I kept in my gun.

"You'll need silver," Cat said. "But not for them."

And the West only got weirder from there.

The Lost Tapes: Future Told

Daniel Arthur Smith

"RECORDING BEGINS WITH today's date, November 30ᵗʰ, 2019. My name is Agent Melissa Muldoon. Present with me is Agent Lawrence Meyer. Commencing interview of one Professor Charles Rampart. Dr. Rampart is a professor of Anthropology at the university and…is this right? You're a psychic?"

"Not really. No."

"But you do claim to have the ability to see into the future?"

"Not 'see,' necessarily. I experience events in and out of time. Past, future, present of course."

"You're a medium then?"

"Uh. Okay. I suppose–if you were to put a label on it–clairvoyant maybe?"

"So you believe you're clairvoyant?"

"Sounds better than time traveler."

"Fair enough. I'll make the correction here in the file…and let's go again. Commencing interview of one Professor Charles Rampart. Dr. Rampart claims to have the clairvoyant ability to see into the future. He has come forward with information regarding a homicide and has agreed to this interview willingly. Mr. Rampart, can you please state your name for the record?"

"Yes…It's Charlie Rampart, Charles, Charles Rampart, but you can call me Charlie. All the kids do. Professor Charlie, they say."

"Thank you for meeting with us. When you called, you stated, in your words, 'you had information pertaining to a murder.'"

"Murders. More than one."

71

"Huh. Again, I'll make a correction in the file. Okay. There. It says that you didn't state to which homicide—homicides—you were referring. Could you please be more specific? For the record."

"These murders, homicides as you call them, haven't occurred yet."

"Excuse me?"

"They haven't happened. Not yet, anyway."

"Is this in reference to a terrorist threat?"

"No, not terrorists. A serial killer."

"How did you come by this information?"

"I've seen them. The homicides, I mean."

"Aha. In the future?"

"Yes."

"Dr. Rampart—"

"Charlie. Please."

"Charlie. If you have reason to believe that someone, or any number of individuals, are in danger, we have to act immediately."

"I understand that. That's why I'm here. It seems the killer is murdering psychics and fortune-tellers."

"All of the victims are clairvoyants, like yourself?"

"Yes. And no. I mean they're not like me, or maybe they are. One is an astrologist, another works as a psychic, and the other two call themselves fortunetellers, but I don't know if they can really experience the future or if they're putting on an act."

"But the commonality is that they are at least perceived as clairvoyant."

"Yes. It is."

"And you believe you're being targeted as well."

"I know I am."

"And how do you know this?"

"I told you. I've seen it."

"And how is that?"

"I'll explain it like this. With the assistance of a chemical cocktail, I'm able to reach an advanced meditative state that allows me to experience what you call the future."

"Chemical cocktail?"

"A mix of DMT and psilocybin."

"Oh. I see."

"I know, I know. It sounds cliché—crazy old anthropology teacher going native. But it's an age-old thing. Shamans and mystics have been performing ritualistic meditation since the dawn of man."

"You wouldn't be the first anthropology professor I've met who's gone native."

"Ha, ha. Get your digs in, but even the Dalai Lama performs a similar practice. Have you ever heard of the Kalachakra?"

"I'm familiar with the Dalai Lama, and the Kalachakra. The wheel of time."

"Yeah. That's right. The Wheel of Time. And do you know what it represents?"

"That's the idea that there's no present without the past or future. But isn't it just an awareness practice, a form of meditation?"

"It's more than that. Have you ever heard of the B-theory of time?"

"Sure. I remember a bit from school. All points in time are equal. As humans, we only experience them in passing. Yada, yada."

"Right. We experience time like a movie. The projector rolls and we take in events in a linear fashion, one at a time, one after another. But if you stopped the projector and pulled the film from the reel, you could see all the frames at once. The past, present, and future, all equal before you."

"Okay. But that's your movie."

"That's right. I can only see my future, my past."

"Then how did you witness these yet to be homicides?"

"I didn't see the act. I saw the crime scene."

"You've seen them after the fact?"

"I'm going to. Yes. You ask'll me about them, and I'll give you the names. You hold me here while you check them out. Everybody seems okay, you think I'm crazy, and then reports of the murders come in the way I'll describe."

"Before you're released?"

"Uhuh."

"You're speaking as if this has already happened."

"To me, to my experience, it has."

"And how will we stop the killer...I mean if the homicides, as you've just stated, are predetermined to happen?"

"We can't stop her. We never could. But we can catch her. In fact, you do."

"When?"

"Why, at my own murder, of course."

"At your murder?"

"Yes. You and Agent Meyer are with me when she attempts to kill me. You catch her in the act. But, unfortunately, too late to save me."

"I see. Can you excuse me for a moment?"

...

"Well, Director Higgins. What do you think? He said he was at the crime scenes. That's practically a confession."

"But he hasn't been there yet?"

"He just admitted he was...or will be."

"Well, we'll contact those people he listed and put them under protection. We'll keep him here on a hold for the next seventy-two hours and restrict his communication."

"You think he's not working alone?"

"He'll have an alibi. If on the remote chance he's right and something does happen, I think you'll take him to the crime scenes as he laid out."

"Why would I do that?"

"To catch the killer, of course. According to him, the killer is going to approach him."

"I guess we'll see."

37

Tales from the CANYONS of the DAMNED

STEVE ODEN   NATHAN M. BEAUCHAMP   SAM OSBORN

IN THE PINK

PRESENTED BY USA TODAY BESTSELLING AUTHOR

DANIEL ARTHUR SMITH

The Moon Sickness
Nathan M. Beauchamp

TANNER CAME DOWN WITH the moon sickness when he was four years old, during Dad's deployment to Saudi Arabia for Desert Storm. I didn't pay much attention to what was going on with my little brother at first, him being so much younger than me. I was focused on how long it would take to kick Saddam's teeth in and get Dad and the rest of his squadron back home. When Tanner came down with the fever days before Halloween, I was too busy watching TV coverage of US airstrikes on Baghdad and dreaming of becoming a pilot to give it much thought. Little kids got sick. Normal enough. Tanner was always hyper-active and broke toys and tossed food off his plate when he didn't like it; him tearing around our farmhouse and throwing stuff at Mom wasn't *that* strange.

Then the screaming started. Wailing, high-pitched and throaty, like an injured animal, loud enough to hear over New Order pumping through my Walkman headphones. Mom forced spoonfuls of Benadryl down Tanner's throat, but it didn't help. The next day, Tanner grew worse and, despite the sickness, devilishly strong, filling the house with inconsolable wailing. He chucked a teakettle straight through the kitchen window and into the backyard. He ground his teeth together so bad, Mom pulled out one of Dad's belts and let Tanner chew it while she held him wrapped in a quilt, rocking him. He bit the belt clean in half. I offered to call Grandpa for help, but Mom wouldn't hear of it. She told me not to call him, or to say anything to any of my teachers or to anyone at church.

Mom managed to get ahold of Dad on Halloween eve. I had my costume laid out and ready: a genuine Air Force flight suit and aviator helmet. Dad had brought it home from Grissom Air Force Base after his last Air National Guard deployment. I'd waited all year to wear it to the harvest festival (that's what they call the Halloween party at the Baptist church), and thought I had a good shot at winning the costume contest. The helmet sat facing me on my dresser, reflective faceplate turned so that I could see the luminous face of the almost-full moon reflecting through my bedroom window. I couldn't sleep. Partly because of excitement, partly because of the moon, and partly because I'd started to get really worried about Tanner. Something was *wrong* with my little brother, something Mom wanted kept a secret.

The phone in the kitchen rang, and I was out of bed in an instant. It had to be Dad. Mom had left messages at Grissom a dozen times, begging them to get him on the line. But he wasn't easy to reach in Saudi Arabia. He and his crew were responsible for loading bombs onto B-1 bombers. Dad told me how they sometimes painted messages on the *ordinance* (Dad always called the bombs ordinance) telling Saddam what they thought of him.

I crept up the dim hallway to the kitchen and stopped in the hall, listening, trying to puzzle out what they were talking about from Mom's half of the conversation. Mom sat at the kitchen table, poring over a calendar and a Farmer's Almanac, cordless phone held in place against her ear by a raised shoulder. Tanner lay across her lap, sleeping. She spoke in an exhausted, worried voice. "It'll be full on November second."

A pause.

"It's too soon. He's too young for this!"

Another pause.

"But you're not here and I don't—"

Tanner lurched awake, clawing at the table and knocking the almanac to the floor.

"It's getting worse." A quiver ran through Mom's voice, like she might burst into tears. I'd heard that same quiver in prior calls when she asked Dad when he would be coming home, and he told her he didn't know, but that it wouldn't be long. "We're kicking Saddam's teeth in," he would say. "We'll be home in no time." I liked imagining Dad loading laser-guided bombs into B-1's, bombs with messages scrawled on their sides, bombs that would fall on Iraqi convoys, breaking Saddam's army. When I heard his scratchy voice coming over the phone from half the planet away, it made me feel proud enough it almost stopped me from missing him so terribly bad.

Mom drew in a shuddery breath, arms cinched around Tanner as he squirmed, sweat clinging to his little, round face. Wiry dark hair curled from his head, much thicker than mine or Mom's. Tanner took after Dad's side of the family.

"I know it's only another few days, but you're not here! You're not the one having to—"

Tanner's mouth opened wide, so wide I could see down his throat. His teeth looked sharper than I remembered. *Did all little kids have teeth that sharp?* He screamed, an animal-keening that filled my stomach with ice water. I must have made a sound too because Mom looked up, catching me eavesdropping in the doorway.

"Go to bed, Jacob."

"I want to talk to Dad."

"It's late, you're not supposed to be up."

"Just let me say hi. Please, Mom?"

Her throat tightened, the tiredness in her eyes deep as the abandoned well behind our barn. "Jacob wants to say hi. Yes, he's awake. No. No. Okay..."

"All right," she said, relenting, "but just for a minute."

She offered me the phone. Tanner's head lunged forward, teeth flashing. They caught Mom on the wrist, breaking her skin, blood oozing out of an open gash. The phone smacked the floor and bounced, double-A batteries flung loose. Mom screamed. I dove for the phone, grasping at batteries, pushing them back into their slots and lifting the receiver to my ear. "Dad?" Dad?"

Nothing but dial tone over the receiver.

Using her uninjured hand, Mom's fingers sunk into Tanner's hair and pulled his head back and away from her body as he thrashed and tried again to bite her. "Jacob, help me."

"How?" I asked, bitterly disappointed that I'd not gotten to talk to Dad, but also terrified of Tanner. His hair wasn't just thick—it had *grown*. And the sounds he was making—

"Help. Me." The heat had drained from Mom's voice, replaced with dull resignation. Her tone knocked me out of my confusion. I leapt to her side.

"Get his legs."

I grasped at Tanner's flailing ankles and managed to snag one of them, but he ripped free a half-second later. A bare heel smashed into my left eye, sending spasms of color across my vision—chartreuse, melon, brilliant pink—the colors of motor oil film in a parking lot after a hard rain. Head spinning, I wrapped Tanner's legs against my chest. He kicked and bucked and shrieked, but I kept a firm hold this time. Mom gripped his wrists and together, we pulled him out between us, his midsection lurching side-to-side, lithe and strong as a viper.

"What are we going to do?" I asked.

"Take him to the barn."

I was breathing too hard to ask what came next. We worked our way to the door, Mom leading, Tanner shrieking. The hair on his head fell around his shoulders. More hair had sprouted on his arms, on the ankles I was struggling to maintain a grip on. His chest had thickened, muscle bunching beneath his damp t-shirt. It looked like it might burst at the seams.

We inched over dew-wet grass under the brilliance of the moon and reached the dairy barn. We don't have a working farm, but Dad wanted to live in the country and liked owning out buildings. We used the barn for storage, and in the summer, Tanner and I built forts in the haymow. Thinking of that Tanner—rambunctious, naughty, curious—made my chest hurt. What had happened to him?

What *would* happen to him?

Neither of us risked loosening our grip on Tanner to flick on the lights. We made our way through dusty darkness, navigating catacombs of stacked cardboard boxes filled with old clothing, Dad's collection of hand-painted Ford Mustang models, Christmas decorations, and things Mom planned to take to Goodwill but never seemed to find the time. Tanner stopped struggling and hung limp between us, his heavy breathing swelling and contracting his chest with panicked rapidity. *He's afraid, too.* All of us terrified, and Dad seven thousand miles away. For the first time since the war broke out, I didn't care about Saddam or his teeth. I wanted my Dad. He would know what to do. He would know how to help Tanner.

"Where are we going?" I asked, voice flat.

"The silo. We can keep him contained there."

Contained. Like Tanner was some kind of virus.

Tanner who didn't look much like Tanner. Hair covered most of his body. Only his face remained free of it, though his jaw had elongated, become pronounced, like the muzzle of a bear. *Or a wolf.* The word jarred something loose in my mind. Tanner's sickness wasn't really a sickness, at least not one a doctor could cure. I refused to think the word, much less speak it. Tanner wasn't anything but Tanner. He was my brother. He would be okay. He had to be okay.

"This way," Mom said, tugging Tanner off to the left and into the small, empty room that connected the barn to the silo. Forty-feet tall and made of concrete slab reinforced by steel rebar, the silo stretched up into blackness. An aluminum cone sealed the top, except for a pie-shaped wedge which could be slid sideways to gain access when the silo was filled with ear corn or soybeans. A man-sized channel ran down the exterior of the silo on the side facing the barn, with removable panels to give incremental access from inside the barn. All these panels were in place except for the lowest one which opened to the interior of the silo. The missing panel lay on the floor, covered in grime, the metal levers that allowed it to be secured in place rusted over. Tanner and I sometimes climbed inside the silo and shouted, listening to reverberating echoes, dancing in the strange shadows cast down from the dome high above. We never stayed long—the stringent odor of old grain fermenting into rancid alcohol drove us away.

"We've got to get him inside," Mom said, eyeing the black, empty hole leading into the silo. "It's going to be tricky."

"What's happening to him?" I asked, fear thickening in my throat.

"Let's get him inside. Then we'll talk."

Tanner had ceased trashing and hung limp between us, panting, sweat clinging to his strange, elongated face.

"Tanner," Mom said, using her calmest, most reasonable voice. "Can you hear me?" Tanner made no sign that he heard, much less understood. I got the sense Mom was speaking to herself as much as to him. "I need you to listen to me, Tanner. We're going to put you in the silo. Just for a few days, until the moon phase changes. Do you understand me?"

Tanner continued to pant.

Moon phase. Mom had been looking at the Farmer's Almanac earlier, checking the phases of the moon. I'd learned about them in school— waxing, waning, gibbous—but the meanings of those words had escaped me. One word and one word only repeated in my mind, over and over, a word I dared not voice. If I said it aloud, it would become true. And when it became true, everything I knew, everything I *thought* I knew about Tanner, my family, the world—would crumble to pieces.

"It's for your safety," Mom said. "You'll be safe in there."

Tanner growled, lips pulling back, revealing his new, long, long teeth. *Canine* teeth.

"Jacob, we need to get him in, head-first. Then I'll put the lowest panel in place and we'll seal the silo closed."

My eyes locked on Mom's bleeding wrist. "What if he tries to come back out?"

Mom tilted her head to the corner of the room where an old cattle prod leaned against the wall. Dad used it on the flocks of Canada Geese that descended on our front lawn every spring and fall. *More humane than shooting them*, he'd said.

"Do you know how to work it?" Mom asked.

"I think so."

"Good. As soon as I start pushing Tanner into the opening, I want you to go and grab it, quick as you can."

Adrenaline ran ice-and-flame through my shaking legs. "Okay." My arms ached from holding my half of Tanner's weight. Whatever we were going to do, we needed to get it done quick.

"You might have to hurt Tanner."

I nodded, jaw clenched to hold back tears threatening to push their way out.

Mom took a deep breath. "Okay. On the count of three, I want you to let Tanner's legs go and get the cattle prod. Here we go. Okay… Three… Two… One…"

I let Tanner's legs drop and sprinted for the cattle prod. The handle always reminded me a bit of Luke's lightsaber in Star Wars. It had a thick, ribbed, metal handle with a push lever to power it on. The handle connected to a three-foot long tube, and at the end of the tube, two pointy electrodes delivered current. I'd seen geese knocked almost unconscious by the prod. I didn't want to use it on Tanner, but I would if I had to.

My hand closed around the cold handle of the prod. I slid the push lever up, and whirled, careful to keep the pointy prongs away from my body. Mom and Tanner looked like they were doing some sort of wild dance, Mom shoving Tanner against the opening of the silo. Tanner clung to the outside of the opening with his hands, clawed feet digging into her midsection, shredding her shirt and cutting the soft skin of her belly.

I shot forward and drove the cattle prod into Tanner's side. It crackled and popped, electric heat singeing hair. Tanner screamed and tumbled sideways. Hit the ground hard. Mom scooped him up, and practically threw him through the opening in the silo. "Keep the prod ready!" she called, reaching for the last wood panel that would seal closed the silo. Tanner and I had only ever lifted it by working together, but we never could manage to force the metal levers down to lock it in place.

Mom groaned, back bent, bringing the panel upright.

A muscular, hair-covered arm shot out of the silo opening, swiping at us.

I held the prod out like a spear, and the next time the arm appeared, I lunged forward, jabbing into the opening. The prongs missed, and I almost fell inside the silo. The prod twisted sideways, wrenched free of my hands for a terrible moment before I latched on with both hands and yanked with all my strength. It pulled free, and I fell backward, spine cracking against the concrete floor. Straining with the panel, Mom lurched and swayed, at last fitting it into place. *Smack*. Tanner crashed against the panel, but Mom held it in place and managed to get first one then the other metal levers pulled, locking it closed.

She slumped against the cold side of the silo. I somehow retained enough presence of mind to find the cattle prod and switch it off. Blood streaked Mom's face. Her wrist had swollen, puffy and purple. Her shirt hung in tatters, the bottom edge of her bra smeared crimson. A long, deep howl came from inside the silo.

"Mom?"

Mom met my gaze. "Yes?"

"Is Tanner... Is he a..."

"No," Mom said, speaking in her "not up for an argument" voice. "He has moon sickness. It runs in your dad's side of the family. Your dad had it too, when he was a boy. It first sets in when a full moon and Halloween overlap."

"Dad had moon sickness?" I asked, then immediately thought of an even more important question. "Did I have it?" I felt certain I would remember if I had, but then, Tanner wasn't in his right mind, and maybe he wouldn't remember any of this once the moon phase

83

changed. I hoped he wouldn't. I didn't want him to have to think about hurting Mom, or me stabbing him with a cattle prod.

"No, you never had it. But according to your dad, it normally comes at the onset of puberty."

"So, I still *could* get it?"

"You could. But I don't think you will. If you were going to get it, you'd have gotten it already. A full moon came right before Halloween two years ago, remember?"

I did remember. My parents had planned a trip to Michigan over Halloween. We'd stayed in a remote cabin on a tiny lake, and I hadn't been able to go to the harvest party or trick or treat. Tanner had been too young to care, but I'd hated every second of that trip because Dad and Mom were so tense and silent. At the time, I thought they'd been fighting. Turns out they'd been watching me, waiting to see if I'd get the moon sickness.

"How long will Tanner have the sickness?" I asked.

"Until the full moon wanes in three days. November third."

"That's a lot of days. How're we going to feed him? Or get him water?"

"From up top," Mom said. "We'll have to climb up the exterior ladder and lower things down." Another ladder ran up the exterior side of the silo—bare, metal rungs bolted to the rebar that held the concrete panels in place. At the very top, a steel platform gave access to the pie-shaped wedge. The exposed ladder filled my mind with thoughts of hands slipping, of tumbling backward, of striking the ground head-first, brains exploding out like an overripe melon.

Muffled thrashing sounds came from inside the silo. Growls and grunts and rasping howls. Three more days. Three days of keeping my moon-sick brother locked in a silo, fed from forty feet above. *What will we feed him? People food? Dog food? Raw meat?* And what would I see when I looked down into the shadowed cylinder of the silo?

"Guess I'm not going to the harvest party," I said.

"Not this year."

I didn't like the party much anyway—I'd have rather gone trick-or-treating and come home with a pillowcase full of good candy instead of the cheap stuff the church handed out—old, hard caramels, candy corn, Tootsie Rolls, peanut butter kisses—all trash. The only thing I would really miss was wearing my pilot helmet and flight suit and winning the costume contest.

Mom held her damaged wrist against her side, in obvious pain. "I have to go into town and get some antibiotics for these bite wounds. You're going to have to stay and watch your brother until I get back."

I nodded with dull resignation and mounting dread. What would happen if Tanner got out of the silo?

"I'll be back as soon as I can. It may take a while depending on how busy they are at the ER."

"What are you going to say happened?"

"Coyote attack."

"They'll call the DNR. Better to say it was a dog, and that it happened somewhere else—somewhere far away, just in case they want to try and find the dog."

"You're right," Mom said, managing a smile despite the pain. "I'm glad you thought of that. You've got a level head, like your dad."

"Are you mad he's not here?" I asked.

"I'm not mad, no. It's not like he had a choice, and he couldn't have predicted that Tanner would get sick so young. It's inconvenient, but the worst is over, and we'll get through this. You and I can manage."

"All right," I said, still afraid, but a bit more hopeful. Mom was right. We'd see this thing through. Dad had a war to fight, and we'd take care of Tanner, together.

Mom hugged me, harder and longer than I could remember, kissed my forehead, and left. The car started, and headlights bore a channel of light through the darkness. I sat with my back against the silo, prod in hand, listening to the choral chirping of crickets. The barn creaked in a rising wind. I realized I hadn't heard anything form inside the silo for a long time. Maybe Tanner had gone to sleep.

I placed my ear against the cold silo wall. If I held my breath, I could just make out subtle scraping sounds. *Digging.* I leapt up in a panic until I remembered the silo had a poured concrete foundation to stop moisture from penetrating from below. Tanner could dig in the surface dirt coating the silo floor, but unless he could claw through the 6-inches of concrete below that, he couldn't get out.

Except when I listened again, the scraping sound seemed to have moved higher. And higher still. Tanner wasn't digging, he was *climbing*. I remembered the claws on his feet and hands, sharp enough slice fabric and tear open skin. Maybe they allowed him to climb the wood panels?

I raced outside and around to the external silo ladder. I slid the prod between my shirt and back, held in place with my jean's waistband, and climbed, rung over rung, until I reached the platform. The harvest moon hung fat and yellow overhead, shining down like a spotlight. Breathing hard, hands sweaty, I held the prod between my knees and pushed the pie-shaped wedge sideways a few inches. I couldn't see anything through the gap. To see anything, I'd have to open it wider. If I did, and Tanner had somehow managed to climb all the way up, he might get loose. I pushed the wedge closed. I wasn't taking any chances. The wedge had no lock, which meant I'd have to stay up here, monitoring the silo's only exit. Chill wind whirled past, cutting through my clothing. I wished I'd brought a flashlight. And a jacket.

I hunkered down on the narrow platform to preserve my warmth and gripped the prod with freezing fingers. How long until Mom would get back? How long until I couldn't stand the cold any longer? I shivered, chest against my thighs, remembering what Mom had said. I had a level head, and we'd get through this.

The shriek of metal grinding against metal shocked me out of a daze of cold and fatigue. I stood up, painful pricks traveling down my numb legs. The wedge had opened. A hairy arm reached through the opening, followed by a rising torso and Tanner's unrecognizable face. Long, white canine teeth flashed below malevolent, blood-orange eyes. I stabbed with the prod but had forgotten to power it on.

Claws raked my arm. The prod tumbled out of my hand and fell. Blood-orange eyes locked on my face. The beast that had once been my brother climbed out of the opening and sat on its haunches atop the curved dome of the silo. It stretched its neck toward the moon and howled. Blood pumped out of the deep slashes in my forearm. I felt dizzy. And tired. So incredibly tired. Only the thought of Mom coming back and the thing getting her gave me the resolve I needed.

"Tanner," I called.

The thing howled, long and angry.

"Tanner!"

The blood-orange eyes turned my direction.

"Come here, Tanner."

The beast moved like liquid shadow, came to the edge of the platform. Two moons shone out of its face. I stood up, face to face with it, not flinching from its hot, stinking breath.

I thought of the pilot uniform sitting on my dresser, and the aviator helmet, and how I'd wanted to one day fly a plane instead of load it full of bombs like Dad. I thought of Mom driving the long way back from the ER, wrist in a sling, wounds bandaged. I wouldn't let anything happen to her.

"I'm sorry, Tanner." I wrapped my arms around his furry body as fangs sank into my shoulder. Pushed forward with all my strength, back into the silo, hugging my brother tight for the last time.

Blind in Battle
Steve Oden

THE OLD MAN'S NEGOTIATIONS sometimes left a bad taste in his mouth.

He tried to never apply personal feelings to a contract. Nor did he develop emotional attachment to an employer or hatred of the opponents whose destruction was his livelihood. The mercenary's code of conduct did not allow any measure of familiarity or dislike. Ignoring this rule was a good way to get yourself killed.

But in this case, he roundly hated his new clients. The young upstarts of the Barony Cadwaller had summoned him—by God, they'd ordered his appearance—to a meeting in a squat, windowless fortress at the lakefront compound controlled by their army of bloodthirsty teenagers.

He was permitted to take a bodyguard with him. They had been forced to submit to the indignity of a full-body search. That rankled, too. Dictating terms to a man of his age and mercenary experience—and with his reputation, to boot!

He looked around the dais where the Baroness Cadwaller's so-called military advisors reclined, slurping alcoholic fruit drinks and crunching salty snacks. Not a one yet showed signs of a beard, and several looked like their bollocks hadn't dropped.

They smoked ganja, spit popcorn and peanuts at the slave toys who served them, and whacked at the motley living creatures with cudgels when they moved too slowly.

The baroness herself, Mistress Elissa, pouted and demanded again to know why he would not allow video drones and spy-crawlers to document the attack and inevitable destruction of rebel detachments in the downtown ruins.

The old man sighed inwardly but gave no outward sign of agitation.

"M'lady, this operation's success depends on surprise. Plain and simple, if they know we are coming and where we plan to strike, they can prepare a counterattack and, heaven forbid, turn the tables. Imagine my brigade taken off the game board and an open road straight into your territory!"

But the baroness was insistent. "We are stronger than the enemy in weaponry and troops. Our fortress walls are thick, and we have air superiority. What can go wrong?"

Smoothing his long beard – more yellow now than white due to gunpowder burns and chemical stains – Santos von Clausewitz glared at the adolescent female with his remaining good eye and hissed through jagged teeth that had torn jugular veins out of the necks of foes in desperate, close-quarters combat.

"Do you remember the disaster in the market district? Isn't this the reason your barony has become foremost along the lake? You declined to join the ill-advised and much publicized military action that the Young Turks Alliance set in motion after trumpeting the impending assault to the high heavens."

Scars covered the empty socket where his left eye had once rested, but the skin puckered pale with anger while his other eye burned neon blue.

"A wise decision, as it turned out. The attack ended in a rout and blood bath for the Turk forces. They were nearly wiped out!" he growled, not adding that indecision instead of any military common sense had blessed the barony in this instance.

"The same thing can happen here if our plans are telegraphed through unnecessary drone and ground-surveillance activity. I realize you want to broadcast the battle for propaganda purposes and morale building. The time to do so is after the fight has been won."

She wasn't accustomed to being lectured by an adult. In fact, Santos wondered if he was the first grown-up with whom Baroness Elissa had ever conversed, let alone plotted military strategy.

"I can order you to accept this as a condition of the contract!" she wailed.

Her advisors stopped abusing the toy slaves and nervously stared at the old man in the tattered red uniform of the First Polar Expeditionary Force.

"Yes, you can." A chilling smile transformed his face. Instead of a cheerful grandfatherly figure, he more closely resembled a hungry feral beast looking for prey.

"I will direct M'lady Cadwaller's attention to what happened the last time someone tried to modify a contract in a way that would put my elves and support echelons at greater risk."

The room remained silent as tears formed in the baroness's eyes and her lower lip trembled.

Santos turned on his heel and marched out of the room, followed by the tall green-skinned biomechanical guard who could have ripped the heads off everyone on the dais with only his bare hands as weapons.

Maybe he should send his bodyguard back to do the deed, but this was not his way of tending to business. These small city district states controlled by adolescents meant lucrative business for good mercenary outfits. Lord knows, the free toys had been on the offensive and winning the fight before real combat veterans had taken the field.

The professionals had proved their worth and now commanded huge payments for services rendered.

The real problem was that the none of the kingdoms warring against the living toys shared information or resources. This was why the rag-tag rebels had not been swept off the field. Why they grew stronger and more aggressive.

He didn't like these jumped-up childish chiggers but would do the job set forth in the contract. The plan was finalized, the units already moving into position. He'd accept no contract modifications or last-minute meddling from the Cadwaller baroness or her idiot military lackeys.

She would learn, once and for all, why his shock troops were called death elves.

The wealth of intelligence information and, for the first time, surfeit of weapons and ammunition should have made him happy, but the blind toy bear felt confused and unsure of himself.

Recently promoted to sector commander, the tattered teddy bear with a killer's instincts couldn't help but wonder how he would keep up with and direct all the units in the coming battle. Why had he agreed to this? His experience was in planning stealthy penetrations and sowing havoc behind enemy lines. He was a leader, but of small teams of elite and deadly specialist toys.

Bear ran his paws over a sculpted battlefield map, wondering where the feint might occur and at what point the real assault would be aimed. Too many scenarios to juggle this time. The enemy had flooded the radio frequencies with chatter and done a good job of confusing his intelligence-gathering section.

He had halted the flow of troops and material that higher-ups at headquarters designated vital to defense of the downtown front. Troopers and units were tripping over one another.

"No answers yet?" he asked, turning unseeing black button eyes in the direction of his staff.

Sock Puppet, her skin stretched like brown crepe fabric, reached a thin arm to move Bear's furry paw south, toward the lakeshore.

"Our best guess at this time is that the breakout will happen in this sector. Most of the buildings have been razed by back-and-forth artillery barrages. There is no defensible high ground. An armored spearhead, properly supported by pre-targeted cannon fire and rocketry, could easily clear a path to the heart of the downtown transportation hub," she said.

They all knew what this meant. Access to the still-standing motorways and bridges would give the attackers quick-strike capability across the city. The rebel defenders might be forced to face battle on multiple fronts.

Toy Soldier interrupted with more bad news. "Our assets embedded in the various district kingdoms along the lake had a hard time getting information out. Either the independent fortress compounds are as much in the dark as we are, or they've clamped down on information as never before."

Soldier grimaced. "None of this has the fingerprints of the youth generals we've become accustomed to facing."

"Opinion?" asked Bear.

Pachy, a miniature elephant dressed in the feathered turban and colorful pantaloons of a Sikh warrior, pointed his trunk at a particular fortress. "Cadwaller, sir. This is where my attention has been focused since rumors came to me of a mercenary commander's presence in meetings with the baroness."

Large ears flapping, he waited for other staffers to contradict him.

"How certain can you be that they've hired outsiders?" Bear could not move chess pieces across the board solely on the basis of gossip and rumors. The toys knew a handful of the kingdoms had hired military advisors, but they'd not been able to temper the bloodthirsty rashness exhibited by the youth armies.

"We can't confirm Pachy's theory, but we have documented the systematic slaughter of toy slaves at Cadwaller in the past week. We lost several of our assets and are basically blind to what is going on inside the barony," reported Soldier.

The old bear's fur was frowsy and mottled with age. Tracks of old wounds formed a network on his chest and muzzle. His staffers were familiar with every scar on his body and loved him for never hesitating to lead from the front, despite the danger.

But this new job required him to make decisions without respect to personal feelings. He'd send living toys to their deaths for the good of the rebellion, and had, but a mistake could mean the end of everything.

In a box on the table were small cast-metal figurines denoting units. In urban warfare, everything depended on proper positioning. Fields of fire and demolitions could balance the rebels' lack of manpower, but a wide front was a challenge to defend without proper advance intelligence.

Bear reached into the box and extracted three of the unit markers. Stubby claws fondled the first: his old scout company. He'd have to send them into danger again. Alone and unsupported. In fact, he feared they'd never survive the mission.

If this gambit worked, he'd need follow-on forces. He put the other figurines on the table, and several of the staffers chuckled. They began to see the shape of his plan.

The remainder of his resources, he'd keep uncommitted until it became clear where the enemy's hammer blow would fall.

He hoped they wouldn't be needed for a fighting retreat.

The assault troop carrier was one of the few stealth reconnaissance vehicles that rebel forces possessed. Relatively light at 20 tons with full combat load-out, the low-slung, six-tired vehicle had an almost silent electric-diesel power plant.

It boasted no cannon turret. Weaponry was limited to a 7.62-millimeter, computer-controlled machine gun and an array of rapid-fire mortars for lobbing anti-personnel bomblets, grenades and smoke cannisters.

Sensors, communication hardware, and transmitters for the vehicle's digital camouflage were contained in pods and blisters on the outer deck and sides, but the overall radar profile was skinny. Heat-dispersing laminate armor ensured a negligible UV shadow but wouldn't stop a high-explosive anti-tank round.

Properly hidden and positioned, the troop carrier—nicknamed "Magic Pony" by her pilot, Fairy Princess Doll—could monitor the enemy's command-and-control networks, gleaning information about deployments, eavesdropping on satellite feeds, even inserting false data packets into the enemy's intelligence-gathering systems.

At the present time, however, the squad assigned to Magic Pony was involved in the boring chore of counting cockroaches.

"Makes me sick, knowing how many of these damned bugs scurry around day and night," said Nutcracker, clacking his formidable jaws in disgust.

Cowboy hooted. "Them insects is out there in the zillions, all right, while we're snug as bugs in a rug in here . . . like a bunch of little Injuns in a teepee."

Big Chief, his squad partner, shook a throwing tomahawk at the gunslinger and frowned.

"For a toy, you are not politically correct! Have you not studied the manual on diversity and relationships among frontline close-combat teams? Oh, I forgot. Cowboys can't read!"

Fairy Princess snorted. Banter between Cowboy and Big Chief reminded her of when she went at it hammer and tongs with Toy Soldier. She missed those days, following the blind bear into hot zones and furious firefights, the team comradery and flirting with the toy she loved more than herself. For all his bluster and bravado, Toy Soldier was the one she achingly missed.

The old team had broken up when Bear was promoted. Her new squad seemed competent but was green, untested. Now they found themselves deep in enemy territory on what might be a wild goose chase or a suicide mission. Really nothing different than past scouting assignments, she conceded.

"Explain to me again why we are counting bugs in this demolished neighborhood?" asked the Nutcracker.

His head was not wooden, like his original namesake. Thick, yes, so Fairy Princess had learned she needed to carefully repeat instructions.

"Cockroach populations tend to increase exponentially in areas where concentrations of combat troops are sheltered. Just look at the reasons: open latrines, garbage everywhere, tons of food scraps. You know how our rations taste and how much goes to waste. Poor personal hygiene, mud, dirt and dust everywhere. Unwashed bodies, corpses, sick soldiers, dirty uniforms, pyramids of rotting supplies, livestock manure. It's cockroach haven, and the bugs are very good at breeding."

Magic Pony had launched several hundred robot roaches to infiltrate colonies and make carapace counts. The data coming in seemed to indicate an unusual spike in populations of the ubiquitous insect.

"Send the data. Let wiser minds than ours extrapolate when there will be enough cockroaches to take over the world," Princess said. "In the meantime, let's ease forward, try to find a pile of debris to hunker behind. I feel like a sitting duck out here."

Santos fumed. His assault elements were in position. They could kick off in two hours. The problem was the damned barony. Their sole contribution to the operation was to demonstrate—not attack—between the grid points he'd chosen for the feint. He wanted to pull the rebel defenders away from the wider front, fool them into thinking they could block the main attack at a carefully chosen choke point.

His plan called for diverting the majority of barony air and artillery assets for bombardment of the faux assault line. When the dust settled, he wanted the rebels to see an army fully deployed and ready to go on the offensive.

"All I requested was a sudden increase in barony radio traffic, concentration of their antique armored vehicles and troop carriers in wide-open spaces, and some wild shooting by untrained troops at non-existent targets. What am I going to get? A stumbling, drunken parade led by pompous teenagers dressed in feathered plumes and gilt finery, with brass bands blaring military marches and a thousand picnicking spectators!"

He clamped his mouth shut. Failure to follow orders on a battlefield was an offense punishable by firing-squad execution. He couldn't very well sentence the mutton-headed baroness to death, however.

This was her silly idea. Instead of a battlefield maneuver, the barony was launching a day-long victory celebration in advance of the real assault. Santos conjectured it was the headstrong girl's way of getting even.

"I should have pulled us out of this circus," he mumbled.

The nearest death elf looked at Santos quizzically, pointed ears perked for an order.

"Never mind, too late now. Get the Brimstone Gutters advance element on the horn for me. I think there's a way to use all the parade confusion to our advantage."

"They're having a what?"

Bear thought he had misunderstood. He was blind but possessed acute hearing. Did his subordinate say what he thought he said?

"A parade, sir. Cadwaller Barony has arrayed military might for what appears to be a celebratory procession through the Gunther Boulevard corridor."

The blind toy scratched his head in consternation. "Is this someone's idea of a joke?" he growled.

His staff stopped what they were doing. Toy Soldier, his operations XO, stepped forward.

"Sorry to report that we have verified the enemy seems to be forming for a victory parade. Their tanks and armored cars are decorated in ribbons and flowers. A grandstand is being erected for VIPs. Troops are dressed in their finest uniforms, and it seems the populace is being furnished large quantities of alcohol and recreational drugs. The baroness herself is slated to speak."

Bear waited while logic blocks slipped into place and his mind modeled a possible explanation. Incredible as it sounded, this had to be the missing puzzle piece for which he'd been searching. But to confirm his suspicions, he had to issue an order that turned his stomach.

"Signal Magic Pony. Tell Fairy Princess I need her to rapidly advance toward the coded grid points in her original orders. Emphasize R-A-P-I-D-L-Y!"

He paused. "What about the cockroach survey?"

"Population's way up, indicative of bugs living off the garbage of a brigade-sized assault force.

"I want Princess to know she will take fire, a lot of it. But her mission is to keep going forward, making noise, and creating as much confusion as possible."

Bear added sadly in a whisper to himself, "And ask her to forgive me."

The digital map in Santos's mobile command center showed an undetected penetration in a weak section of the rebel's defense perimeter. He had ordered the stealthy advance of a death-elf probing force, including sappers and grenadiers. Their orders were to plant landmines and demolition charges along the most likely routes that the toy forces would use to funnel reserves into the fight.

He intended to use the racket caused by those Cadwaller fools to drive several daggers into the opposition, then enlarge the most damaging cut into a broader front from which to release an armored blitzkrieg.

Things were shaping up nicely, after all. Plus, he'd experienced another epiphany. After the First Polar Expeditionary Force had rolled up the rebellious living toys, they'd reverse field and attack the Cadwallers.

He'd always wanted his own kingdom.

"Say what?"

Nutcracker had just dismounted to cut several enemy communication cables with his powerful, chomping jaws. Big Chief was at the ultra-low frequency radio linked back to headquarters. He held up a broad hand for silence.

"Orders, not coded! It's going out on all bands, no attempt to hide it."

He stared at Princess and shook his head. "Attack. We are supposed to rapidly advance with all guns blazing. Emphasis on rapid."

Princess hollered, "Tell Nut-head to get his ass back in here. Lock and load. Start broadcasting the jamming signals. Turn up the digital camo to make us look like a land dreadnought with twin railguns. We're coming into town to kick ass and drink their whiskey!"

The comms buzzed angrily. Signals section suddenly found itself flooded with incoming assistance appeals.

"Reports, numerous reports of a battalion-strength attack against our forward elements. The free toys figured out our movements and laid a trap!" cried the alarmed colonel who sat at the monitor next to Santos.

The old man unbuckled his holster flap and pulled the pistol. He calmly pumped a round through the panicked officer's head. No one objected as the body toppled. Conduct unbecoming a death elf.

"I need to know what's really happening. Somebody, get me on the line with a unit commander out there."

In ten seconds, a patch put him through to a grenadier captain.

"Lots of firing and explosions. Our radio traffic monitor picked up an in-the-clear rebel order for all forces to attack. That's all I know, sir."

Santos considered whether the free toys had been tipped to his strategy by the Cadwallers. It was possible. They partied while his elves died. Oh, they'd take a lot of rebels with them, but what was left of his brigade would be a negligible force. The damned traitorous kids would mop them up then run the toys to ground themselves.

No wonder they were celebrating victory, curse them!

He had to recall his advance forces and form a defensive hedgehog, with weapons pointed ahead and behind. The barony would discover that death elves with their backs to the wall were nasty foes.

"Jehu be my witness, the Cadwallers will rue the day they sold out the First Polar Expeditionary Force," Santos swore.

Under the pavilion, Baroness Cadwaller, appareled in silk pajama bottoms and a jeweled bikini top, pointed to the munitions exploding in the ruined metropolis. Santos was hard at work and soon, the hated rebel toys would be squashed.

She was stoned and already bored. This was not as exciting as she had hoped. Even with the background noise of rumbling tanks on parade and the far-off blasts of cannons and aerial bomb explosions—even while she savored the mental image of disobedient toys being blown to smithereens—the petulant child princess sought more excitement.

So, she had arranged to have living toy slaves hacked to death by members of her advisory council. Blood was always satisfying. The sound of sharp swords slashing flesh, the cries of mortally wounded servants. These were the sensory pleasures that never failed to please her.

The bladed weapons had been distributed. She rose from her throne and stepped toward the first slave. The sword was reassuringly heavy in her hands. She raised it for the death blow. To her drug-addled brain, it seemed that the intended victim, a Kewpie doll, screamed too early. She hadn't made the first cut. Everyone was screaming, in fact. Why?

Cadwaller Barony had erupted in panic. Her advisors dropped their swords and fled, some falling in the stampede of soldiers and civilians. One of the battle tanks in front of the grandstand, painted mauve with yellow ribbons drooping from the main gun, blew apart in a gout of fire and smoke. Pieces of red-hot metal whirled through the crowd, taking off heads and legs.

Toward the lakefront, twinkles stood out against the shadowy fortress. She heard bullets whiz and strike bodies. More explosions surrounded her. "We're under attack," she dully realized.

"The mercenaries have betrayed us. Santos von Clausewitz turned traitor!" the Baroness Elissa screamed.

Out of the cloud of dust, a tall, green-skinned figure appeared. The old geezer must have sent a death elf on an assassination mission.

Instead of Santo's bodyguard as she'd expected, she beheld a scaled, two-legged beast with protuberant eyes and jaws filled with hooked teeth. It dripped with water and moss from the lake. Powerful arms held a rocket-propelled anti-tank weapon.

"Miz Cadwaller, I presume? My name is Cap'n Croco of the Free Toys Amphibious Task Force. Our ships are currently parked in the harbor, and we control your installation back there."

The thing jerked a clawed thumb toward the fortress, over which a mushroom cloud of swirling embers rose.

From the pall of smoke and ashes, another free toy marched. This one was clad in colorful robes and pantaloons, curved knives hooked on a gem-studded belt and a heavy revolver in its blunt-fingered hand.

Unfurling a long gray trunk covered in tattoos, Pachy nodded to the baroness and said, "Madam, you are our prisoner. You will undoubtedly will be executed for war crimes and the massacre of innocents. I would like to shoot you between the eyes right now, but my orders do not allow it."

But the baroness didn't hear. She had fainted dead away and lay in a heap, snoring loudly.

Santos stood without bodyguards in the wrecked debris of his mobile command center. The red uniform coat trimmed in white ermine was gone, blown off in the concussive blast of a heavy-caliber howitzer shell.

He was a pitiful figure, bare chested with sallow, saggy skin and pendulous man breasts. Most of his beard had been blackened or jerked out by the roots to keep his face from burning. He'd lost a combat boot, and his droopy-bottomed red pants were held up by a piece of frayed rope.

His lone blue eye had dulled in defeat, but he held himself stiffly at attention.

Of course, Bear could not actually see him, but he heard other members of his staff snicker impolitely as the commander of what formerly had been known as the First Polar Expeditionary Force tendered his unconditional surrender.

"You fully understand and agree with the terms?" asked the toy bear.

Tears seeped from the old man's single eye. "Yes, and I am grateful that you have chosen to spare my surviving elves."

Toy Soldier stepped to Bear's side. "They are brave warriors. You are to be commended for their training and loyalty."

Santos nodded sadly. "I only wish my former employer had recognized those battlefield virtues."

"Ah, yes. This brings up another point of discussion," Soldier said.

"You realize, of course, that the Barony of Cadwaller no longer exists. Your contract has been made null and void. If our understanding is correct about the set of rules under which mercenary forces operate, the Free Toys now have the option of assuming your contract until reparations have been made to offset our military expenses from the battle."

Santos sighed. "That is an accurate interpretation."

"Commander Santos, we want to reconstitute your brigade and put it to better use than the late and unlamented Baroness Cadwaller," Bear said. "You'll work for us now."

After a surprised intake of breath, the old man straightened his spine and saluted.

"You honor me and my elves, sir."

Soldier saw the mercenary leader's shiver and called an aide to bring a coat. On the sleeves was the insignia of the Free Toys. Not as snazzy as the red uniform suit he'd previously worn, but as Santos held it up his blue eye twinkled.

Sewn to the back of the coat was a new unit designation: "League of Free Elves, Col. Santos von Clausewitz commanding."

Duty that the blind bear had been dreading could not be put off any longer. The search-and-rescue team had found the burned hulk of Magic Pony almost inside the perimeter of a death elves' forward artillery battery. How the lightly armed and armored scout vehicle had made it this far was a mystery.

Princess had dismounted her combat squad when the troop carrier's camouflage screens blinked offline permanently due to nearby electromagnetic warhead explosions. The Indian chief and Nutcracker survived, both seriously wounded. The others were dead heroes.

Magic Pony plunged through a firestorm, causing much more disturbance than a single light reconnaissance vehicle should have. In fact, the enemy had been fooled into thinking they faced a major assault force. This one act of bravery had turned the battle.

Santos von Clausewitz had reacted like Bear had hoped he would, pulling in his units and going on the defensive. This allowed the Free Toys commander to release the Crocodile Fleet's assault boats and landing craft for a surprise attack on the Cadwaller fortress.

Afterward, it had been a bloody mop-up—and a search hinged on hope that the scouts had survived. Forlorn hope, as it turned out.

Bear had ordered that her body remain in the blasted wreckage of Magic Pony. He intended to make this place a shrine. If peace was ever achieved between former slave toys and the human monsters who created and corrupted them, Bear wanted to return here and remember Fairy Princess's sacrifice.

The sobs were quiet, but the blind bear had good ears. Toy Soldier's chest heaved. He mourned the lost heroine who'd meant so much more to him. They had loved one another, not just as combat brothers and sisters. It went deeper.

The toy bear didn't know how to comfort his XO and friend. He felt too much guilt.

"I am the one who sent her in harm's way. I am the one who knew she would never return," Bear whispered to his subordinate. "I killed her and the others."

This was the moment when Toy Soldier beheld Bear's sorrowful face and understood. For the first time, he realized the aching burden of command, new curses laid on his leader's heart with each skirmish, battle and victory.

Blind bears can cry, and plastic buttons can't hide the tears.

The Rat
Sam Osborn

GEORGE WOULD HAVE NEVER recognized her if it wasn't for the rat. This was Wednesday at the liquor store. She had a bottle of wine gripped by the neck and was headed for the register. Customers stared as she passed; children pointed. Anne had always snared the attention of passersby.

George didn't remember her being quite so tall, though. Her hair was different, too.

Straight now, thicker. But how many women, even in the city, walked around with a pet rat? He supposed it was possible that it wasn't her. Probably more pet rats in the city than he preferred to imagine.

He watched her from three aisles over. She stepped into line.

If she lived in the neighborhood, he thought...*had just moved in.* George could show her around, catch up on the years since they'd called it quits.

He looked down at his shopping basket, at the lonely bottle of whiskey rolling around. The cheap stuff, and a lot of it. He left his aisle and stepped toward the line at the register.

A few customers stood between them. Not being a tall man, George craned to see past them to the black woolen shoulder with a feminine curve where a rat sat sniffing at the air. He checked his breath, swallowed, and poked his head out from the line.

"Uh, Anne?"

She didn't turn around, not at first. The other customers did—the man between them in line, the cashier, a woman browsing at the counter. They all looked up as though their own names were Anne Huff and had each dated him, George Heussler, for two mostly good years after college. They hadn't. But she—the she with the rat—turned around after that first excruciating moment and immediately George realized that he had been mistaken. This woman's eyes were green and they looked at him with utter confusion. This wasn't Anne with the brown eyes, gripping a tankard of wine—port, he now saw—but some other woman entirely.

"Sorry. I thought you were someone I knew. Sorry."

He waved at her, desperate for everyone to just carry on. The rat sniffed at him from its perch. It scampered behind the woman's neck and reappeared on her opposite shoulder, haunches straddling her purse strap. Its pink tail, just as ropy and perversely anatomical as George remembered, hung around her neck like a scarf.

"George? George Heussler? Is that you?"

So it *was* her.

"Jesus, Anne, I barely recognized you. You look so—so different."

She grinned, looking through the customers standing between them. "Good, I hope?"

"Yes, sorry. You look great. I'm just—it's actually you. Here."

She stepped out of line and reached out for a hug, which was how George found himself nose to nose with the rat. Its pink nose twitched, sniffing at him.

"I see you and Henry are still a pair."

She patted the rat's head. "My constant companion."

She really didn't look much like he'd remembered her, but now that he thought about it, that wasn't such a bad thing. He wouldn't say Anne's less-flattering features—the narrow set of her eyes, the wad of skin under her chin—were what had precipitated their breakup, but they were all he could see at the end. This Anne had no such flaws. *Probably different chinks in the paint,* he thought, *new ones I can't yet see.*

God knew George hadn't improved his own image much. He seemed to be shrinking when he looked in the mirror most mornings, an effect of his life compressing around him. The world had gotten ole' Georgie by the balls as of late. Surveying Anne now and noting her improvements, he was suddenly very conscious of what his hair looked like.

"Listen," she said. "You wanna check out and find someplace to drink all this booze? Got a lot to catch up on."

She reached for his whiskey and placed it on the counter.

"You don't have to do that," he told her.

She shrugged. "I want to show off. Call it a peace offering."

They walked through the neighborhood more slowly than he'd walked those streets in a long time. It felt good to show someone around, to point out the shops and eateries that comprised his life. He'd been all right in the years since they'd parted, found a good neighborhood and stuck with it. Work wasn't difficult, but he'd allowed it to spill over into life's margins. He came home late, ate at his desk, checked emails as soon as he woke in the morning. In some corner of his mind he knew that he was waiting for someone to provide for, someone to lead him back into the light of the real world. And here was Anne, moving in six blocks away; moving in alone.

He suggested a coffee shop, then suggested a bar, but she insisted on showing him her new place. It was empty, she said. The movers were due to arrive the next morning. Just an inflatable mattress and her suitcase, basically.

As they walked, Anne kept hinting at a relationship that had turned sour. Something long-term that had showed promise. She'd had a string of lousy luck since they'd split, a claim George found difficult to believe as he looked her up and down from the corner of his eye. She didn't look like the sort of woman who had any trouble finding suitable partners. That was the old Anne—his Anne—a quaint sort of beauty. This Anne was something else. It was like walking around with Anne's taller, leaner, funnier sister.

Henry the rat had stayed the same, though. He had to be almost ten by now. George sifted through his knowledge of rodents to figure their life expectancy. The query didn't yield much.

If he was being honest, George had never taken to Henry. He doubted if many of Anne's boyfriends had. She'd insisted, though. Said it calmed her to keep an animal around—to be a creature's protector. Henry didn't complain. If he wasn't tucked into her purse, the rat was perched up on her shoulder, spectating her world and drawing rictuses of disgust from passersby.

If it was a kitten or even, say, a ferret, it wouldn't have been so off-putting. But a rat. Rats were a far cry from mice, George realized soon after he'd met Henry. You could feel sorry for a mouse you'd vowed to kill once it had been caught in a trap behind the oven. Mice were no more than furred pinecones with trim tails and button noses. Rats were another story. The furred pinecone turned to a matted log when you climbed up the food chain from mouse to rat. Beady eyes turned to red spheres, button noses turned to buck-toothed fangs. And their tails. Not trim so much as…intestinal. They were endless, those tails.

Yes, George thought, that was a nasty quirk of Anne's that she hadn't shaken. In its own way, the rat defined her—the single trait that proved it really was Anne leading him back to her digs for some polite, no-nonsense humping.

His neighborhood was what magazine writers had come to label as "gentrified." Slick condo high-rises mingled with the rundown vinyl-sided numbers that they were rapidly replacing. Generations of immigrant families displaced by upper-middle class interlopers like himself. It didn't bother George so much, likely because he was on the winning side of the equation.

He thought of this only because Anne was leading him away from the antiseptic heart of his economically adjusted neighborhood. Six blocks away was apparently one block too far. The streetlights were clicking on as night fell and only a scant few of the bulbs illuminating her street still worked. *It's rare,* George thought, *to find a street so dark in the city anymore.*

"Fire damage," she said. "It's why the place is such a deal."

She nodded to a trio of buildings burnt down to their steel framework.

"Mine's the next one over. Plenty of smoke damage but it's all fixable. They let me move in now for free, basically, as they do the renovations."

"Huh," George said, trying to remember back to any fire.

"Don't let the looks put you off. You're not gonna believe the space."

It was when she turned to climb the steps of her stoop that he saw it: streaked along the back of her coat were thick lines of rat shit. George saw that the wool coat was stained with the stuff. Fresh Henry droppings mixed with the faded streaks of shit left behind from past laundry cycles.

Henry swiveled his head toward George just then, his eyes trained on the man as if to indicate that he was proud of this scatalogical history; like it proved his dominance over that particular territory.

Those red eyes looked right into George's as another turd tumbled down Anne's back. George suddenly wished he was back home, sitting alone with his whiskey and cable television.

"Got the lights working last night," Anne said.

"Oh," he said, trying to clear his mind. "Nice work."

She didn't use a key to enter the building so much as she shoulder-checked the front door until it dragged itself out of her way. She flicked a switch and a hanging construction lamp shuddered on.

"The third floor's kaputz but the first two floors are a-okay."

He forced a smile.

"Safer than a carnie ferris-wheel," she said as she started up the stairs. "Kidding. They're fine."

The thing about the stairways and halls of apartment buildings is that they were an underserved element of urban dwelling. As a child who'd been raised in a collection of tidy suburban neighborhoods, the hallways of friends whose parents inhabited apartments were all uniformly terrifying. If vagrants and escaped asylum occupants weren't behind those mold-streaked doors, then a waifish she-ghost with an overabundance of teeth no doubt lurked there. As he grew older, George realized that the vast majority of apartment buildings, no matter their cost, sported dank, dubious hallways. It was a fact of life he'd come to terms with, like taxes and laundromats. And so, it wasn't until they reached the door of Anne's unit that George realized that something was truly wrong.

Put simply, there was no door. Hers was the fifth of a dozen units that lined the second-floor hall. Though none of the units seemed occupied, Anne's had the distinction of being the only apartment accessible to anyone—squatters, dealers, pimps, and all manner of urban boogiemen—with enough moxy to call it their own.

"How much did you say you were paying?"

"It's criminal how little I got it for."

She'd hung a blanket over the door, which she now held aside for him to pass through. He stepped into a hazy darkness. Sodium halogen light seeped through blankets hung over the windows.

"Just a sec."

She stepped past him and fumbled in the dark. A Coleman camp lantern took a glow. "So?"

So. She isn't homeless after all. Her story checked out, it seemed. A stack of lumpen moving boxes dominated the room, pinch-hitting as a coffee table, bedside stand, and stools. An ancient turntable was wired up. A few records were scattered beside a half-deflated blow-up mattress. She'd bought flowers and had stuffed them into empty wine bottles to give the place a decorated vibe that vaguely reminded him of community theater.

Romantic, in a gypsy sort of way. She returned from the kitchen with two glass jars and a saucer, the bottle of port tucked under her arm. Henry scuttled after her.

"Henry's a port fiend," she said. "If you can believe it."

She poured them a round. They clinked glasses. Henry set two front paws on the saucer's rim and started lapping up the thick wine.

"That won't hurt him?"

"I've stopped asking questions. Henry knows what he wants."

She smiled the "you know boys" look moms give. George hadn't gotten a chance to look at her head-on all night. They'd been walking shoulder to shoulder, Henry between them. But now he got to see her on full display, curled up on a blanket in the soft glow of the lantern, a bottle of booze set between them and a record waiting on the turntable. He swirled his port, thinking that he ought to be feeling the warm anticipation of low-stakes, familiar sex. Instead, his stomach was clenched. He felt uncomfortably alert.

It was her eyes. *A woman's eyes don't change.* But it wasn't just the color. His Anne had looked at him with the patient knowledge of a woman who knew she deserved better. This Anne was peering at him through the vacant eyes of a child. This Anne was a stranger. How had he not seen it before?

Anne hopped to her feet and went to the turntable. She had been saying all the right things, laughing about old times, catching George up on friends he'd lost touch with. She had been Anne. But this woman he looked at now—he became sure as she turned around and the first notes of a song (appropriately heavy on the theremin) started playing—was a woman he'd never met.

Henry looked up from his saucer, sniffed in George's direction. His snout was stained purple.

Anne sat down again, took a sip of her drink, and undid the top two buttons of her blouse.

Those empty green eyes bore into him.

"I'm curious to hear what you've been up to all this time," she said. "I've been dominating the conversation."

"Oh, um. I bounced around a bit from job to job after moving here. But I've, you know, settled in and been at my current gig for a few years now."

"Not work, dummy. Girls. What about the women in your life?"

"As in plural? Like multiple women?"

She laughed. It was an automatic laugh, like a command that had been programmed in.

"Not many women, to be honest. A few short things here and there. But nothing…"

"Nothing like us?"

George looked at her over his glass of port, which he now found himself draining. "Well, I guess. That was such a long time ago."

Anne emptied her own glass and shrugged. She undid another button of her blouse and held out her hand. George flinched to reach for it, but not before Henry pattered up to her fingers and crawled aboard, scampering back up to her shoulder. His saucer of port had been emptied.

"Little fucker can hold his wine," George choked out, his throat suddenly parched.

"What about friends?" she asked.

He shrugged.

"I play basketball every once in a while with a few guys. Pickup games. But, you know, I try to stay social. Couple work friends."

Henry turned a circle on Anne's shoulder and settled upon his haunches. They stared at George. George took a sip of his drink, forgetting it was empty. Nobody blinked.

"And your sister, did she ever move out east?"

George shook his head. "Nope. Settled down with someone. They're living in Boise, I think. Last I checked."

She nodded, satisfied with this line of questioning, and looked down at Henry upon her shoulder. Henry hadn't moved. The rodent's red eyes were planted on George.

The genetic similarity between rats and humans was becoming apparent.

George suddenly felt like he'd fallen a few links down the food chain.

The vacant look in Anne's eyes worsened. Her pupils were tiny dots in those big green pools, as though she had retreated deep within her own body. Her eyes weren't vacant so much as evicted.

Her mouth opened once again and a voice came out. As she spoke, George became certain that he was no longer listening to Anne. It was Anne's voice that he was hearing, this stranger who called herself Anne, but George was struck with a gut-level knowledge that it was Henry who was speaking.

"I'm so glad I ran into you, George. It's been, what, eight years?"

The lights cast by the lantern left many shadows around the apartment. George sensed movement in all of them—a scurrying along the walls.

"You wouldn't believe the places I've been," the voice said through Anne's mouth. "Wouldn't believe the people we've been."

A line of blood slipped from Anne's right nostril. The moving boxes began to shift.

"It takes a lot of work to raise a family these days," it said.

Henry the rat turned and looked up at Anne. The woman began to quake. Her eyes, now bloodshot, were no longer vacant. There was the abject terror of captured prey inside them.

Those eyes pleaded for help. Henry looked back to George.

"You seem to have a good grip on things, George. You've done well for yourself since we've left you."

George nodded dumbly. There was a scratching from the record on the turntable. The moving box beneath it had shaken, its lumpen nature moving inside.

"I want us to…" Henry stroked a whisker, thinking. "I'd like to give it another go with you. You seem like a natural-born provider."

George froze, still holding his empty glass—he finally managed to shake his head. *No, please no,* he tried to communicate.

"And you know how it gets," the words now vibrated coarsely from Anne's mouth. "So many mouths to feed."

Henry stepped from Anne's shoulder. As his tail slid along her chest and down her lap, she collapsed along with it. Anne fell, an inert puppet, to the hardwood floor.

The final thought George had, springing crazily into his mind as Henry stepped across the blanket between he and Anne, was that the unit's hardwood flooring would look terrific after a good polish. She really had found a good deal with this apartment. And he supposed, as briefly as it took for Henry to hop the final eight inches of flooring onto his lap, that George himself was a good fixer-upper. That he would perform just fine after a good polish. A twinge of flattery coursed through his synapses just then, as George realized that he was being evaluated for a partnership after all. Or, maybe more accurately, evaluated for seaworthiness as a competent vessel.

As that last morsel of conscious thought slipped past, George's mind was gripped by something dark and massive. He lost control of his limbs and peered through his own eyes like a man staring through a ship's porthole. His pupils contracted and through those far away points of light he watched as a thousand rats slipped from their hiding places to feed on the stranger he'd mistaken for Anne.

The Lost Tapes:
The Rain Man
Daniel Arthur Smith

"RECORDING BEGINS WITH TODAY'S date, March 4th, 2020. My name is Agent Melissa Muldoon. Present with me is Agent Lawrence Meyer. Commencing interview of Dennis Matheson regarding the disappearance of his family while at their cabin on Arrow Lake. Mr. Matheson, we were notified about the disappearance by the local police and we're here today at their invitation. I want to make it clear that we're here to listen and to help. I realize that this can be overwhelming, so if at any time you need a break, or anything at all, just say so."

"I appreciate that."

"Could you please state your name for the record?"

"It's Dennis Matheson."

"Thank you, Mr. Matheson.

"They think I did it, don't they?"

"They?"

"Jimmy Chambers, the police, they think I had something to do with it."

"I assure you, for the safety of yourself and your family, that every option is evaluated. No stone left unturned, if you will."

"Of course. Yeah. Of course."

"And with that in mind, I encourage you to share anything you think could help. We won't take long. Agent Meyer wants to get out of here before the rain comes. We have a drive ahead of us and it's supposed to be another downpour."

"That's when it comes."

"It?"

"The Rain Man."

"The Rain Man?"

"That's what Irena called it."

"Your daughter?"

"Yeah. Anyway, whatever it's called, that's when it will come. Just like the old man and the kid said it would—and they were right. It will follow the rain."

"The old man from the country store?"

"Yeah. We always stop there on the way to the cabin. Pick up milk, juice–gas-up–that sort of thing. There was a storm coming when we stopped the last time, and a light drizzle when I gassed up. When I finished, I went inside to pay for the gas and grab the milk and juice like I always do. The kid was at the register and the old man was sitting in his rocker at the end of the counter next to the little TV, same as every time I see him, but this time he was upset."

"Upset?"

"Yeah. He was shaking a bony finger at the little TV, rattling off something in Lithuanian to the kid—"

"You speak Lithuanian?"

"No, no. I couldn't understand a word, but his grandson said that's what it was, and that I needed to hurry on my way because he had to lock up. It was just after three, so I asked him why he was closing up so early, and he told me that it'd be best if we got home before the rain, because that's when it comes."

"It?"

"Yeah. I kinda laughed, told him I didn't think we were going to make it, beat the rain I mean, but the old man didn't think it was funny. He lifted himself out of his chair, leaned over the counter then, very serious like, says in broken English, 'Go home. Go home now. Before it comes. Then stay inside. It will follow the rain.'"

"They were concerned?"

"Yeah. You could say that. They couldn't get me out of there quick enough—bolted the door behind me."

"You went home, home being the cabin."

"Well. That's where we were going anyway. But we didn't beat the rain. I'd barely made it into the car and out of the parking lot when the sky went black. The first big drops fell, quarter sized splats across the windshield, then just as quickly it went full buckets. It was coming down thick as a fog, I could barely see a car length ahead of me...Then..."

"Then?"

"That's when we first saw it."

"The rain man?"

"Yeah. But I didn't know it at the time."

"Uh-huh. Just what did you see?"

"Like I said, the rain was coming down in buckets. The wipers were flashing across the windshield, but didn't make much difference. Then from out of nowhere there was something in the road—"

"Something?"

"Something–yeah–came out of nowhere."

"Can you describe what you saw?"

"Well, like I said, the rain was thick, all I could see was a tall, dark, inky figure—could have been a man or a moose walking toward us, I couldn't tell—but it was tall. One minute I was telling my wife Ellie about the old man and the next, I was slamming the brakes. We hydroplaned, swerved, went into a spin. I thought we were going to fly off the road."

"Did you hit it?"

"Yeah. I think so. I mean, there was a thump."

"And did you fly off the road?"

"No. No we didn't. Sheer luck. It was hectic, though. We did a few donuts then slowed to a stop. It was the freakiest thing. The world's flying by at a million miles an hour, and then everything went silent— except for the rain drumming on the roof. Eerie. I checked Ellie and the kids. They were shook up, but okay, so I opened the door to get out of the car. Ellie handed me a magazine she had on her lap and told me to hold it over my head."

"Did you find anything?"

"A small dent on the back quarter panel, but nothing on the road. Keep in mind the rain was still coming down by the bucket. In fact, when I stepped around the side of the car, a truck appeared from nowhere, horn blaring, barely missed me, about threw me out of my skin. Anyway, I was soaked when I got back into the car. My wife, Ellie, asked me the same thing, if I'd found anything, and I told her it was probably a deer. Which probably wasn't the wisest thing."

"Why's that?"

"Because right then, she got worked up. Her and Irena were afraid it was hurt and wanted to go after it. I told them it was fine, just scared, bounced right off, probably a mile away already and that we'd never find it."

"Did you believe what you told them?"

"Maybe I did then. I don't now."

"Why do you believe what you saw in the road was related to what you saw later?"

"Because of the eyes."

"The eyes?"

"Yeah. Glowing lemon yellow, like the sun. It had had eyes like that."

"Most likely the reflection of your headlights. Cows, deer, cats, dogs, they all have a reflective layer behind the eyes to help them see in the dark. It's called a tapetum lucidum—makes their eyes glow when a light hits them."

"Yeah, except I saw them out my driver's side window when we swerved toward it. Two lemon yellowed suns…anyways, at the time I thought it might be a deer. Wasn't 'til I saw him again that I knew better."

"And that was at your cabin."

"Yes. It was dusk. The rain had stopped and I was stoking the fire when Irena and Billy ran into the room to tell me that the rain man was outside. I followed them to the window, and sure enough there he was, all in black, standing in the middle of the two-track at the edge of the mist, those yellow orbs bright as midday, staring at the cabin."

"And you're sure it was the same man you say you hit with the car?"

"Oh yeah. Strangest thing. Even then, out in the yard, he looked inky, out of focus."

"The police report says that you didn't confront him."

"I took the kids into the kitchen with Ellie, she took them upstairs and then I went back to the door, but he was already gone. I mean, he wasn't still standing in the middle of the two-track, but I knew he had to be out there. We're the only cabin at that end of the lake and that two-track drive is almost a mile long. There's one other cabin near the main road, but it's abandoned, roof falling in. So even though I didn't see him, I knew he was out there somewhere."

"So what did you do?"

"What could I do? I grabbed the axe off the porch, locked the doors and windows, then called Jimmy Chambers, told him we had a prowler."

"Officer Chambers said that when you called him, you were quite upset."

"Wouldn't you be?"

"Undoubtably. He said that he did drive out there, and when he arrived, he found you sitting on the ground in front of the cabin, your axe in hand. He said, and I'm reading this directly, 'Mr. Matheson was sitting with his back against the edge of his porch. He was barefoot, staring out into the woods, and clutching a single edged axe close to his chest. He appeared to be in shock and did not respond when I spoke to him. The front door was open, so I unholstered my side arm and entered the house. Upon my search, I did not find anyone else on the premises.'"

"No. There wasn't anyone else. It took them."

"You saw the rain man take your family?"

"No. I heard them, though. The screams. My wife, my son and daughter. Screaming for their lives. Calling out. Begging me to help. I ran for them but before I reached the top of the stairs they'd stopped screaming. I went looking room to room, not sure what I'd find, but they'd disappeared. All I found was a pool of water in the kids' room."

"I see. So you didn't actually see the man in the cabin?"

"No. But who else could it be? I figure we got his attention when he hit him on the road, so he followed us out the to the lake, followed the rain just like the old man and the kid said."

"Where do you think he took them?"

"I don't know. I looked around the house. I called out for them…But…I couldn't find them."

"Mr. Matheson, I have to ask, do you know why he didn't take you?"

"No…No I don't…"

"Okay Mr. Matheson, that's enough for today. The orderlies are here to take you back to your room. You'll be comfortable there."

"And what about my family? Are you going to find them?'

"I assure you, Mr. Matheson, we'll do our best."

ABOUT THE AUTHORS

Wendy Nikel is a speculative fiction author with a degree in elementary education, a fondness for road trips, and a terrible habit of forgetting where she's left her cup of tea. Her short fiction has been published by *Fantastic Stories of the Imagination, Daily Science Fiction, Nature: Futures,* and elsewhere. Her series of time travel novellas, beginning with *The Continuum,* was published by World Weaver Press in 2018-2019.

For news and updates visit wendynikel.com.

Gordon B. White words has lived in North Carolina, New York, and the Pacific Northwest. His debut fiction collection, *As Summer's Mask Slips and Other Disruptions* (Trepedatio Press), is forthcoming in January 2020. A graduate of the Clarion West Writing Workshop (2017), his fiction has appeared in venues such as *Pseudopod, Daily Science Fiction,* and the Bram Stoker Award® winning anthology *Borderlands 6*.

Gordon also contributes reviews and interviews to outlets including *The Outer Dark podcast, Nightmare Magazine, Lightspeed Magazine,* and *Hellnotes*.

For news and updates visit gordonbwhite.com.

KJ Kabza, a has written and sold over 70 short stories to a multitude of anthologies and award-winning fantasy and science fiction magazines. His debut print collection, *The Ramshead Algorithm and Other Stories*, has been called "a fresh new voice in the genre" by Booklist and "bursting with both ideas and emotion" by RT Book Reviews.

Steve Oden has worked in the publishing industry–mainly newspapers and magazines–for more than 30 years. Although retired, he provides editorial services on a consulting basis, mainly to corporate clients, and writes on assignment. His newspaper columns have appeared regularly in Tennessee and Alabama publications since 1980, winning awards from the Alabama Press Association, University of Tennessee-Tennessee Press Association, Society of Professional Journalists, National Rural Electric Cooperative Association and several wildlife conservation organizations.

K.H. Vaughan a refugee from academia with a Ph.D. in clinical psychology. In his other life he taught, published, and practiced in various settings, with particular interest in decision theory, forensic psychology, psychopathology, and methodology. He lives with his wife and three children in New England. He is an editor emeritus with Dark Discoveries Magazine and Hellnotes.com and writes speculative fiction including horror, science fiction, and fantasy.

His official webpage can be found at www.khvaughan.net, and he is also on Facebook.

Kevin Lauderdale written essays and articles for the *Los Angeles Times*, *The Dictionary of American Biography*, and **McSweeneys.net**. His short fiction has appeared in several of Pocket Books' *Star Trek* anthologies as well as various small press publications. His story "Box 27" was published in the science journal *Nature*. This is his fourth appearance in Canyons of the Damned. He hosts the Old Time Radio podcast, *"Presenting the Transcription Feature,"* and co-hosts *"Temple of Bad,"* the podcast about movies that are so bad, they're practically a religious experience, both on the Chronic Rift network. He is a member of SFWA and HWA.

Nathan M. Beauchamp started writing stories at nine years old and never stopped. From his first grisly tales about carnivorous catfish, mole detectives, and cyborg housecats, his interests have always delved into strange waters. Nathan works in finance so that he can support his habit of putting words together in the hope that someone will read them. His hobbies include reading, photography, arguing for sport, and pondering the eventual heat death of the universe. He has published many short stories in magazines and anthologies and holds an MFA in creative writing from Western State. He lives in Colorado with his wife and two young boys. Nathan co-created the award winning YA science fiction series **Universe Eventual** where he writes as N.J. Tanger. The series includes **Chimera, Helios,** and **Ceres** and the prequel **Ascension. Universe Eventual** is available on Amazon.

Sam Osborn is a Mexican-American filmmaker who has directed films for **Topic Studios, Vice News, Great Big Story, Jazz at Lincoln Center, Vox, GQ** and more. Most recently he completed the first season of **Eating,** an ongoing documentary series for **Topic Studios,** along with the four-part documentary series **Night Shift**. The pilot episode of the interactive digital series **Language Keepers** premiered at the **Smithsonian National Museum of the American Indian** and was supported by **the Alaska Humanities Fund** and the **National Endowment for the Humanities.** He's currently completing work on his debut feature-length documentary, **Universe**.

His official webpage can be found at samdavidosborn.com.

Jessica West (a.k.a. West1Jess) is currently pursuing a state of self-induced psychosis, also known as writing. In the past, she has worked for Wal-Mart, a lawyer, and a bank. Now if she could just get a couple years experience with the IRS and the NSA, world domination is in the bag.

Jess lives in Acadiana with three daughters still young enough to think she's cool and a husband who knows better but likes her anyway.

For news and updates visit west1jess.com

Daniel Arthur Smith is a USA Today bestselling author. His titles include *Spectral Shift*, *Hugh Howey Lives*, *The Cathari Treasure*, *The Somali Deception*, and a few other novels and short stories. He also curates the phenomenal short fiction series *Tales from the Canyons of the Damned* and *Frontiers of Speculative Fiction*.

He was raised in Michigan and graduated from Western Michigan University where he studied philosophy, with focus on cognitive science, meta-physics, and comparative religion. He began his career as a bartender, barista, poetry house proprietor, teacher, and then became a technologist and futurist for the Fortune 100 across the Americas and Europe.

Daniel has traveled to over 300 cities in 22 countries, residing in Los Angeles, Kalamazoo, Prague, Crete, and now writes in Manhattan where he lives with his wife and young sons.

For news and updates visit danielarthursmith.com